"Abigail," *he murmured*

Ever so gently, he slipped one hand beneath the baby's back and head. Lord, she was tiny. So tiny she practically fit within his palm. She stared at him with great solemn eyes and blinked her lush lashes. Then she heaved a mighty yawn for one so tiny and fell instantly asleep. Carefully placing the sleeping baby back in her bassinet, he brushed a finger across the downy crown of her auburn-tufted head. "Little Abigail."

Dani eyed him curiously. "Is that a family name?"

"No, it's...just a name."

"Nick?" A curious flush tinted Dani's cheeks. "Thank you for everything. The wedding and getting me to the hospital in time. And...and being there when I needed you."

"You're welcome." He hesitated, unwilling to leave until he'd rectified one final omission. "I did forget something, though."

"What's that?"

"I never had the opportunity to kiss the bride."

Welcome to Whirlwind Weddings!

Dear Reader,

This is a brand-new miniseries about matrimony, featuring strong, irresistible heroes, feisty heroines and four marriages made not so much in heaven as in a hurry!

When the authors came up with the idea for WHIRLWIND WEDDINGS, we gave them just one stipulation: their heroes and heroines had to meet and marry within a week! Mission impossible? Well, a lot can happen in seven days....

Titles in this series are:

January	*Marry in Haste* *by* HEATHER ALLISON
February	*Dash to the Altar* *by* RUTH JEAN DALE
March	**The Twenty-Four-Hour Bride** *by* **DAY LECLAIRE**
April	*Married in a Moment* *by* JESSICA STEELE

Day Leclaire says: "My husband and I were married five short months after we met, in our very own Whirlwind Wedding. It was a total fiasco! We'd planned to elope. We really did. One small problem: I made the mistake of telling my parents ahead of time. Well...they didn't take kindly to that idea. Not at all. So instead of running off to Vegas? We had to 'elope' to Illinois where they were living and get married there! And then they made us do it a second time six months later, so all our relatives could attend. Nineteen happy years later, we're still laughing about it!"

Day Leclaire

The Twenty-Four-Hour Bride

Whirlwind
Weddings

Harlequin Books

TORONTO • NEW YORK • LONDON
AMSTERDAM • PARIS • SYDNEY • HAMBURG
STOCKHOLM • ATHENS • TOKYO • MILAN
MADRID • WARSAW • BUDAPEST • AUCKLAND

Special thanks to Bonnee Pierson for trying to keep me
within the realm of "computer reality."
And all my appreciation to my CompuServe "buds."
You guys are great!

ISBN 0-373-03495-4

THE TWENTY-FOUR-HOUR BRIDE

First North American Publication 1998.

Copyright © 1998 by Day Totton Smith.

Printed in U.S.A.

PROLOGUE

NICK COLTER left Paris two full weeks ahead of schedule.

He didn't know what drove him. It was an impulsive, gut-level decision based on emotion rather than intellect. It was also totally out of character for a man nicknamed Ice—as totally out of character as the one night he'd last allowed instinct to override common sense.

The night he'd made Dani Sheraton his.

A strong instinct for self-preservation fought to deny the impact of that one unforgettable evening, fought to keep him from resurrecting the memory. Not that it did any good. All the willpower in the world couldn't change hard, cold fact.

He'd gone to Dani the night before he'd left for Europe. He'd taken her into his arms and later into his bed. And after five long years of waiting, he'd finally made love to her.

Then he'd left.

But the memories of that brief moment persisted, haunting him day and night. It didn't take much. A flash of ink-black eyes in Rome. Dusky curls caressing a creamy shoulder during a layover in Madrid. A husky, feminine laugh in the middle of a business meeting in London. And instantly he'd find himself transported back in time.

He'd see Dani standing in front of his granite fireplace, slowly disrobing, stripping away piece by agonizing piece of rose-red satin. And as each delicate garment fell, more and more of the woman within was unveiled.

She'd been so full of warmth, her heat seeping beneath his icy guard, bringing the rebirth of spring to a man who'd spent a lifetime in barren winter.

She'd knelt at his side, firelight licking across her skin and catching in her heavy, dark curls. He'd never wanted a woman as much as he'd wanted her—not before and not since. Still, he'd been cautious, careful. He remembered how serious her expression had been. She'd seemed almost hesitant—which was ridiculous. He'd never known anyone as confident and outgoing as Dani. But that night...

Perhaps she'd been haunted by memories of her own, because that night she'd changed from the wild gypsy he'd always known to a creature of shy passion and almost virginal uncertainty. And when he'd joined with her, she'd stared at him with huge, stunned eyes, as though she'd discovered some wondrous secret that had been kept hidden from her until that moment. The image had burned its way into his heart and soul, pursuing him across two continents and through more months than he cared to remember.

He closed his eyes, finally realizing what drove him to leave Paris. It crystalized into a stark, inescapable certainty. It was time to return home.

Dani needed him.

CHAPTER ONE

"YOU'RE PREGNANT."

Dani gripped the front doorknob, wrath vying with a crippling pain so intense it threatened to bring her to her knees. Anger won, giving her the strength she needed. She glared at Nick, furious that not a flicker of emotion dimmed the brilliance of his flinty blue eyes. As usual, he remained cold as ice while she needed every ounce of restraint to keep from going up in flames.

"You have a talent for stating the glaringly obvious," she snapped, splaying a protective hand across her extended belly. She'd been a fool to think she wouldn't feel anything for Nick when they next met. If anything, her longing had grown with each passing month until it had reached staggering proportions. How was that possible, when he clearly felt nothing? "You're right. I'm pregnant."

"How far along are you?" He didn't wait for a response, but shook his head, shards of September sunlight darting through the white-blond streaks. It gave her a wrenching pang to recall that the last time she'd seen him it had been moonlight ricocheting off those pale streaks, frosting his hair with silver icicles. "Never mind. I already know. Nine months."

Denying the truth was pointless. "Almost to the day."

"Which means it's my baby."

"Brilliant observation, Sherlock." It wasn't her wittiest comeback, but it would have to do, considering Nick had banged on her door without so much as a phone call to warn of his return.

Of course, if he *had* called, she'd have made a run for it. Or at least a waddle for it, which was about as fast as she could move these days. She just couldn't face the consequences of her actions from that long-ago night. Nor could she face the knowledge that once again she'd given herself—heart and soul—to a man incapable of love. She shot him a wary glance.

Why, oh, why did he have to catch her now, when she was totally off guard? Why couldn't he have come home in two more weeks, as planned? In another few days, she'd have given birth and... And what? In the endless months since he'd left, she'd never quite figured out what would come after that momentous occasion. She grimaced, conceding an undeniable fact of life. As usual she'd allowed her late husband's personal motto to make her decision—why plan tomorrow when it can be left to chance?

She stood before Nick, torn between wanting and fleeing, the want far outweighing the urge for flight.

"Why don't you let me in while you work on your explanation," he suggested mildly.

Dani folded her arms across her chest, refusing to budge. "I don't need to come up with an explanation."

To her utter amazement, a tiny spark of fire ignited those cool blue eyes. "Yes, sweetheart. I'm afraid you do. Now, are you going to deactivate the alarm system and let me in?"

"No."

He didn't ask again, but simply eased her to one side and stepped across the threshold. Instantly an alarm sounded.

"System override," he snapped. "Colter zero-zero-one. Cancel alarm, Gem."

"ALARM CANCELLED, MR. COLTER." The

sweetly feminine voice issued from hidden speakers. "RESET SYSTEM?"

"Affirmative."

There was a momentary pause and then Gem announced, "SYSTEM RESET IN PROGRESS. ALARM REACTIVATED FOR ZONE ONE. WELCOME HOME, MR. COLTER."

"Dammit, Nick!" Dani protested. "Why is she welcoming *you* home? This is my house and my security system."

"Perhaps it's a glitch in the programming."

"Not likely, considering you designed the thing."

"Enough, Dani." A wintry chill settled across his features, and she felt an anxious pang. "I didn't come here to talk about Gem, as you damn well know. You can't avoid discussing the real issue any longer."

"What issue is that?" she asked as blandly as she could manage.

"The baby." His mouth twisted. "Or had you forgotten?"

Forgotten? She pressed a hand to her stomach. How could she when every day she felt her baby's sweet life fluttering within her?

Every tiny kick provided a constant reminder of that one delirious night with the man currently towering above her. She'd dreaded this meeting, uncertain of how a man of ice would take to impending fatherhood. "I haven't forgotten a darned thing. As for avoiding a discussion of the future..." She set her jaw, apprehension filling her at the thought of a future that included Nick Colter. "I'd be quite happy to avoid that discussion for days. Weeks. Maybe even months."

"Not a chance, sweetheart. We're going to resolve the matter here and now."

She knew that tone, knew she wouldn't be able to hold

him off much longer. Still, she could try. "First, explain how you got in here. How were you able to override the security codes? You shouldn't be able to do that!" She faced an intimidating bank of digital readouts on a panel by the front door. "You may not allow Mr. Colter in without my authorization! You got that, you mechanical hunk of junk?"

"PLEASE USE APPROPRIATE FORM OF ADDRESS WHEN MAKING A REQUEST," came the melodious response.

Dani gritted her teeth. "Mr. Colter isn't allowed in here, Gem. No more overrides without my permission. Got that?"

"AUTHORIZATION CODE?" Gem requested crisply.

"Oh, hell. Um, three-eight-nine-eight-six-seven-four. I think."

"AUTHORIZATION OH - HELL - UM - THREE EIGHT - NINE - EIGHT - SIX - SEVEN - FOUR - I - THINK REFUSED. ERROR NUMBER FOUR - THIRTEEN. PLEASE FORMULATE REQUEST ACCORDING TO APPROPRIATE GUIDELINES. HAVE A GOOD DAY, MRS. SHERATON."

She whipped around to face Nick. "What the devil does that mean?"

"It means you can't override my override."

"Why not?"

"You don't have the proper authorization codes."

"Then give them to me."

"Why? They won't do you any good."

She glared impotently. He had her with that one. She didn't have a clue when it came to mechanical monsters like Gem. "I could try. You never know, I might get lucky."

The slightest smile touched his mouth. "Your partic-

ular brand of luck is likely to get you mistaken for a
burglar and hauled off to jail again.''

''That was Gem's fault. I forgot my card, and she
wouldn't accept my voice code.'' She shook an accusing
finger at the digital display. ''She called the police on
purpose!''

''Gem's a machine, Dani. She was simply following
her programming when she alerted the authorities.''

''Then why did she laugh?''

''It was a hiccup in her voice modulator. The error
was with an earlier model. Her programming's been up-
graded several times since then.'' His explanation
sounded far too smooth. ''But if it makes you feel any
better I plan to give Gem a full overhaul later this week.
We can't afford any computer errors with a baby on the
way.''

''Just make sure you take out that override while
you're at it.''

''Not a chance.'' He changed the subject with typical
decisiveness. ''Where would you like to talk? Kitchen
or living room?''

''My office.''

If she'd hoped to get a rise out of him, she failed. As
usual. He simply inclined his head and motioned for her
to proceed.

She'd chosen the office because it would offer some
small advantage for what would undoubtedly prove to
be a difficult conversation. She'd hoped to hide behind
the desk and let him play the part of a client or visi-
tor—not that the desk would hide much of her current
bulk. Nor, she suspected, would he willingly play any
part she chose to assign him. He never had in the past,
a fact that had always aggravated her no end.

Nick gestured down the hallway. ''Lead the way.''

He followed as Dani started toward her office, fighting

to regain the pieces of his almost nonexistent self-control. A baby. His hands clenched. Heaven help him, Dani carried his child, bearing the priceless burden with an innate feminine grace. Pregnancy gave a gentle sway to her hips, a rhythmic rock and roll that held his attention with frightening ease. It didn't matter that the final stages of pregnancy were upon her. As far as he was concerned, she was the most beautiful woman he'd ever known. Her hair appeared glossier than he remembered, thicker, curling past her shoulders in heavy black waves. And her skin radiated a translucent quality, as though lit from within. It took every ounce of self-possession not to reach for her, to keep himself from pulling her into his arms and claiming all that should be his. Only one thing kept him from touching her.

She hadn't told him about the baby. He'd had to find that out on his own. For nine long months, she'd kept it a secret. There could only be one explanation. She didn't want him in her life. His mouth firmed, and he forced back an unsettling combination of fury and panic. Too bad. Whether she liked it or not, he intended to be a major player in her future—and in his child's. He wouldn't be shut out.

"When exactly is the baby due?" he asked the moment they entered the office.

"Any day."

Determination filled him. "Then there won't be much time."

Dani eased into the leather chair behind her desk and eyed him suspiciously. "Much time for what?"

"To get married."

His comment shouldn't have surprised her. She'd known Nick for five impossible years, knew how persistent he was. She'd also learned through painful experience that once he made up his mind about something, he couldn't be budged. Which meant she'd better hurry and dissuade him before his latest idea became fixed in concrete.

"I don't want to get married again. Once was enough."

"Once to Peter was enough. I'm not Peter."

No, he wasn't. In fact, the two men shared absolutely no resemblance whatsoever. Peter Sheraton, her high-school sweetheart, had been boyish, charming and slyly persuasive. He'd also been totally untrustworthy. Nick, on the other hand, wouldn't know charm if it slugged him in the jaw. And as for being persuasive... No doubt his idea of that particular trait involved the use of a bulldozer with its throttle thrown wide open.

"Look, I know this situation comes as a surprise—"

"We're getting married."

"But once you have a chance to get accustomed to the idea," she continued doggedly, "I'm sure you can come to terms with it."

"No doubt. Once we're married I'll have, what? Two or three whole days to come to terms with it?"

She winced at his sarcasm. As for having two or three days... "Only if you're lucky," she muttered. On her visit to the doctor that morning, he'd used the words "any minute" rather than "any day."

"I'd have had a hell of a lot longer if you'd told me last month. Or two months ago. Or even six or seven months ago."

She cleared her throat. "Yes, well—"

"Why didn't you let me know?" he cut her off coldly.

"There's a really good reason."

"Which is?"

She lifted her chin. How could she explain how much she wanted him—and how much she feared that desire? How could she explain her instinctive awareness that once he knew about the baby he'd try to take control of her life—and her child? She couldn't deal with that. She simply couldn't. "I didn't want to tell you."

Was it her imagination that made her think he flinched? "Why?" he demanded.

"Because I knew you'd insist on doing something foolish. This only confirms it."

"Foolish," he repeated softly. "Foolish, like what? Like giving my child a name?"

"The baby has a name! My name."

Where in the world had she ever gotten the impression that his emotions were on ice? One look warned that she'd made a huge mistake. He started toward her, his long strides devouring the distance with nerve-racking speed.

Planting his hands on the desktop, he leaned across it. "Wrong. It's Peter's name my child will bear. And if you think for one minute I'm going to allow that to happen, you're dead wrong."

She hadn't thought of that. She honestly hadn't. "We can legally change it."

"That won't be necessary. When he comes into this world he'll already bear my name."

"She."

"What?"

"The baby. It could be a she."

"Fine with me. She, he and all the ones that follow will be Colters. I don't intend to negotiate on this point."

All the ones that follow? She swallowed. No. No way.

She'd suspected he'd do this once he found out about the baby, suspected he'd sweep into her life with demands and conditions, forcing her to examine and acknowledge feelings she'd kept safely locked away for almost a year. "I don't plan to negotiate, either. I'm not—I repeat *not*—going to marry you. Got it?"

"We'll go to the county courthouse and apply for a license first thing in the morning. You choose whether we take our vows before a judge or a minister. I can live with either one."

"You're not listening to me."

"By tomorrow night we'll be man and wife."

"Stop it, Nick!" She stumbled to her feet. "Just stop it. I'm not marrying you or anyone else, and that's final. Don't you get it? I never want to marry again."

He drew back as though he'd just realized how aggressive his stance had become. His eyes narrowed as he considered her expression. "You may not want to marry again but you have a responsibility to the child you carry that outweighs your personal desires."

She shook her head in instant denial. "Lots of single women raise their children without benefit of a father."

"Not when the father is ready, willing and able to contribute his fair share."

Heaven help her, she'd never won a verbal battle with him before. But this time would be different. For sanity's sake, it *had* to be. "We're already business partners. That's quite enough, thanks."

"You're sidestepping the issue. Our partnership has nothing to do with the baby or its conception." He lifted an eyebrow. "Does it?"

"You know it doesn't." She shot him an apprehensive glance. This probably wasn't the best time to broach her next problem. Still… If it got him off the subject of marriage, she'd risk it. "As long as we're talking about Security Systems International—"

"We weren't. We were talking about our child."

"Well, now we're talking about SSI," she persisted. "And I think you should know that I've reached a decision. I want you to buy me out."

The change in him was instantaneous. One moment

his eyes were alive with fierce intent, and the next the life force behind that cobalt glare winked out of existence. All expression was bleached from the taut planes of his face. "Why?"

"Peter was the one interested in SSI, not me. After all, you and my father-in-law started the business. I just came along for the ride."

"You're an important part of the firm."

"I've never understood about computers and security systems. You know that. Besides, I'm of no use to you or the company. It seems pointless to continue."

"Peter wasn't computer literate, either."

She heard the criticism behind the comment and chose to ignore it. The two men had argued at length about that particular fact.

And as much as she hated to admit it, Nick was right. A man owning half of a computer security system should, at the very least, have a working knowledge of computers. "Granted, Peter didn't have your expertise, but he was a born salesman. He brought in a lot of clients."

"Wrong. *You* brought in the clients. They listened to you, not Peter."

"I can't believe we're arguing about this. I seem to remember your offering to buy us out on a fairly regular basis."

"An offer Peter always rejected."

She gazed at him steadily. "I won't be rejecting this offer."

Nick folded his arms across his chest with a finality she couldn't mistake. "That's because I won't be making one."

"I don't understand. For years you encouraged us to sell our interest in SSI." Frustration edged her voice. "Now you want me to stay? Why?"

He shrugged nonchalantly, but she noticed the taut play of muscles that ridged his shoulders and tightened his jaw. Tension rippled just beneath that impassive exterior, she'd stake her share of the business on it. "I need you," he stated with devastating simplicity.

She smiled in genuine amusement. "You don't need anyone."

He acknowledged her observation with a wry nod. "So I've always been told. Nevertheless, I need you. At least for now."

"Why?"

To her surprise he began to pace. It left her with an uneasy feeling. Nick never paced. He never made unnecessary gestures, never allowed his expression to betray his emotions. And he never, ever permitted an adversary a glimpse of any possible vulnerabilities—assuming he had any. And yet... He paced, revealing with distressing clarity his inner turmoil.

How utterly un-Nick-like.

As though he was aware of her thoughts, his restless movements stilled, and an impenetrable calm cloaked his thoughts. "The truth is, I've spent almost a year overseas restructuring our international division. Unfortunately it's caused me to neglect our domestic clients."

"How does that—"

"We have competition now. Serious competition. I'm surprised you haven't noticed."

"I've been preoccupied," she stated with a touch of irony. "I know we've lost a few clients, but—"

"And we stand to lose even more if we don't put a lot of time and effort into recovering that business. You're invaluable when it comes to wooing clients."

She gestured downward. "I'm not in a position to woo

anyone. I'm about to have a baby, in case you didn't notice.''

"Oh, I noticed.''

The soft timbre of his voice worried her. It always had.

Whereas Peter would frequently erupt in a volcanic display of fury, she'd never seen Nick lose his infamous calm. Instead, he grew progressively quieter, his husky voice dropping to a rumbling murmur that was far more intimidating than any of Peter's explosive tantrums.

"Well, if you noticed, then you must realize that I don't have a lot of time to put into SSI right now.''

"I won't need a lot of your time.'' He frowned. "Why the sudden urgency to sell? It's been almost two years since Peter died. What's happened to prompt all this?''

Dani hesitated, uncertain how much to tell him. He was so analytical, so logical, so shrewd. How could she confess her innermost longings to him? It would be like explaining emotions to Gem. "It's time I got on with my life,'' she finally answered. "I'd like to sell this monstrosity Peter called a house and buy something cozier. And I'm thinking that I might...well, that I might start up a business.''

"You already have a business.''

"It was never mine, and you know it. You and my father-in-law got it off the ground. And though Peter and I attempted to step into his shoes when he was killed—'' She fixed Nick with a candid look. "They were shoes neither of us adequately filled.''

"How are you going to start up a business and care for a newborn when continuing at SSI is too much for you?'' he asked with aggravating—and all too typical—logic.

"Obviously I won't,'' she conceded. "Not at first.''

"Then until our baby is born and you're ready to begin this new venture, you can continue with our company.''

Our baby. *Our* company. She suspected he used the word deliberately to weave a connection between them, a connection she longed to break. She fought to control her irritation, rubbing the ache building in the small of her back. "Do you think we could discuss this later? I'm rather tired."

He was at her side in two seconds flat, a supportive hand beneath her elbow. "Sit down, Dani. Try to relax."

"That's a little difficult at the moment," she retorted.

"That's only because you're making the situation more complicated than necessary." Before she had time to argue, he asked, "When did you last see a doctor?"

"This morning."

"No complications, I assume?"

"None."

He hunkered down beside her, his keen gaze level with her own. She'd missed him, she realized with a pang. Missed his concern and kindness, his sharp intelligence and calming influence. The panic she'd experienced when he'd first appeared faded, replaced by the tentative stirring of emotions she refused to name.

"You haven't been sleeping, have you?"

"It's been difficult," she confessed. "It doesn't seem to matter how many pillows I use or where I put them, I can't get comfortable."

"It won't be much longer," he said consolingly.

If only he wasn't so close. It brought back memories, memories she'd spent nine long months struggling to excise. The fact that she'd been totally unsuccessful only served to fuel her discomfort. It didn't matter that Nick cloaked himself in the trappings of civilization or that his crisp white shirt and Frank Lloyd Wright inspired tie lent credence to the illusion. Nor did it matter that he possessed the logic of a computer and kept his emotions harbored snug within the polar ice caps. She knew the truth.

One touch gave him absolute power over women.

"You're thinking about that night."

His words were whisper soft, slipping beneath her defenses and summoning a series of images she'd long ago banned from her memory. That night! Why couldn't she forget? It was New Year's Eve, and she'd gone to his house to deliver some papers she'd found locked in Peter's personal safe—financial documents she thought Nick would need. At his request, she'd waited while he'd studied them.

Apparently, he hadn't been any more successful at deciphering the jumble of figures and handwritten comments than she. Although judging by the frown that lined his brow, the parts he'd managed to assess hadn't pleased him. After a full half hour of silence he'd carefully set the papers aside. But instead of showing her to the door, he'd tossed a log on the fire and turned on the stereo. Next he'd offered her a glass of champagne, and then...

And then the clock had chimed twelve.

"It's New Year's," Nick had said with an odd smile. "Why don't we start it off right?"

So Dani had found herself in his arms, exchanging a quick, friendly kiss. She'd been particularly vulnerable that night, or so she'd told herself. After all, it was the anniversary of Peter's death—a full year to the night since he'd announced his intention to divorce her. A full year since he'd walked out the door, climbed into his Lotus and then proceeded to wrap the car around a telephone pole. Nick would be leaving in a few short hours for Europe. And she'd felt so alone, anchorless. At least that's how she'd rationalized matters when the morning sun had arrived, returning with it her sanity.

But that one kiss had astonished her. Nick's mouth had been firm and determined, tasting of champagne and passion. It definitely hadn't been in keeping with a man nicknamed Ice. The contradiction intrigued her, tempted her to sample his mouth again and then again. He'd given everything she'd asked of him with each escalating kiss—and more. Far more, as it turned out.

To be brutally honest, she hadn't thought about consequences that night. Other thoughts occupied her mind. From quick, friendly kisses to lingering, heated exchanges, they'd slipped swiftly toward a burning, hungry demand. His dress shirt and tie angered her, and she'd stripped the silk from around his neck before tackling the buttons.

"Do you always dress this formally when you're at home alone?" she'd demanded.

"Not usually. I was out earlier."

"Let me guess. Business, right?"

A bitter chill crept into his eyes. "What else is there?"

His comment inexplicably angered her, just as it filled her with a painful sadness. "Let me show you what else."

A reckless determination seized her, stealing the last of her reserve—and common sense. He didn't protest as she plucked his gold cuff links from their holes and swept the shirt from his shoulders. If anything, she sensed his amusement—and something else. Not vulnerability. No, not Nick. But there was an odd hesitancy about him, a caution she'd never before associated with his decisive nature. She remembered wanting to analyze it, wanting to question him about it. Unfortunately, she'd become distracted at that point, perhaps because what she'd discovered hidden beneath his crisp white shirt had so astonished her.

She'd found the broadest shoulders she'd ever seen on a man. The muscles were beautifully shaped, carved into clean, utterly masculine lines. She couldn't believe she'd never noticed them before. How could she have missed something this impressive? His skin gleamed like golden cypress, full of light and warmth and begging to be caressed. She pulled back ever so slightly, allowing firelight to lick across his corded biceps, watching in fascination as it curled into his furred chest.

She reached for him, tracing a path from his shoulders to where the pelt of dark brown hair began. The color was such an unexpected and striking contrast to the white-blond streaks capping his head. Yet even more fascinating was the abrasive texture. It stirred a delicious tingle across the surface of her palms, a tingle she'd never gotten from Peter's boyishly smooth skin. She stroked Nick's chest, unable to resist. And all the while, inch by agonizing inch, her fingers dipped ever lower, following an enticing path that led past the flat, rippling plane of his abdomen straight to his belt buckle.

There he stopped her. "Are you sure this is what you want? There's still time to change your mind."

"No. I'm afraid there's not. It's now or never."

"Don't start something you don't plan to finish," he warned roughly.

Perhaps if she hadn't been so impulsive, she'd have listened. But all she heard was the need seeping from beneath his harsh tones. And she responded to that desperate call with all her heart.

She left his arms and stood close to the fire. And while he watched with eyes hotter than the bluest star, she stripped away her black dress, followed by scraps of rose-red satin. Finally, all that remained was the clip that held her hair in place. Kneeling at his side, she discarded even that. Her hair had fallen past her shoulders in a heavy curtain of thick, dark waves, curling across his knee. And still he didn't move.

"Nick?" she'd murmured uncertainly.

"Please. Don't let this be an illusion."

She hadn't known how to answer his whispered plea. Not that she needed to. Nick drew her close and held her with such a devastating combination of urgent passion and gentle concern that she'd wept. And what had followed had changed her. Utterly and completely. His lovemaking had revealed a wondrous secret—a secret that had been kept from her all the years of her marriage to Peter.

Nick had shown her the true meaning of love.

"You can't forget that night, either, can you?" he asked quietly.

Dani closed her eyes, fighting to bury the memories. Not that she'd succeed. At least, she never had before. "I can't forget the next morning, either." Disillusionment had set in that day, when she'd woken to a cold, empty bed and a lover long gone.

"I had no choice but to leave. You know that."

"I don't want to discuss it!" she retorted with an edge of despair. "The entire episode was an aberration."

"That *aberration* created our child."

It was her turn to flinch. She curled a protective hand around her stomach. "I didn't mean—"

"Didn't you?"

"No! I want this baby."

He didn't miss a beat. "So do I."

She couldn't mistake his sincerity. It came through in every word he uttered. Unfortunately, she'd spent the last nine months thinking of the baby as hers. It came as a distinct shock to realize that he might have similar emotions. Her mouth curved in a whimsical smile. Nick experiencing emotions? Now there was a peculiar thought—as peculiar as believing Gem could feel.

"It would seem we have a small problem on our hands," she stated.

"Not at all. I've already given you the solution."

"Marriage."

His gaze remained rock steady. "Marriage."

"And if I don't agree?"

His expression turned implacable. "You will. You don't have any choice."

"There are always choices," she insisted.

"Not this time, sweetheart." The endearment sounded more natural than she'd have thought possible. "You want me to buy out your share of the partnership. You also want to start your own business. You can't do either without my agreement and cooperation."

She couldn't believe it. Not of Nick. She regarded him numbly. "And the price of your agreement is marriage?"

CHAPTER TWO

IF NICK FELT ANY REGRET at forcing her hand, he didn't show it. Instead, he inclined his head as coolly as though he'd just proposed she take bleu cheese on her salad instead of ranch dressing. "One year of your time," he said. "That's all I'm asking. You help firm up our domestic sales, and on the baby's first birthday, I'll buy you out if that's what you still want."

"And our marriage?"

He didn't answer, and Dani studied him in frustration, wishing she could read him as easily as he seemed to read her. But in the five years they'd been partners, she'd never successfully deciphered his thoughts. This time proved no different.

"You can't keep what you never had," he replied cryptically.

"Give it to me in English, Colter. Will you agree to a divorce?"

"You can leave after a year. Just promise you won't go far."

"You're asking me to stay in San Francisco?"

"I want my son or daughter close by." His eyes narrowed. "Is that so much to ask?"

Yes! She caught the word at the last possible instant, but he must have read her thoughts. Again. A wealth of bitterness dawned in his gaze, and with a small sigh, she shook her head. "I'm sorry. I'm not trying to be difficult, but you've caught me off guard."

"That makes two of us."

"I know," she whispered. "It's just... You're making demands—"

"Reasonable demands."

"No, they're not! Not to me." She closed her eyes, fighting for composure, fighting to stem the tears that came with such ease these days. "Dammit, Nick. This wasn't supposed to happen."

"But it did. Whether you like it or not, you're having my baby."

From his crouched position beside her, he reached out to cup his child. He paused at the last possible instant, his hands hovering a fraction above the taut curve of her stomach. She glanced at him questioningly, and her breath caught at his expression. For a brief instant his mask of indifference tore open, exposing such bitter-sweet longing, the tears she'd fought to suppress blurred her vision. In that split second she recognized his deep-seated urge to touch their baby, to feel the life growing within her womb. The next moment a more customary calm iced his features.

He pulled back, about to drop his arms to his side, when she impulsively caught his hands and pressed them tight against her ripe belly. He'd never have asked, never have taken without consent. And yet she knew, *knew*, that more than anything in this world, he wanted to feel their baby's life force pulsing beneath his hands. He gritted his teeth, thick, sun-kissed lashes sweeping downward to conceal the fierce blue light gathering in his eyes. Ever so gently he shifted his large hands across the ripe expanse of her pregnancy, the heat of his touch spreading a delicious warmth straight through to her womb.

"The baby tends to be active at this time of the day," she whispered.

No sooner had she spoken than he captured several

hearty kicks within his palm. He gave a startled exclamation. "That's the baby?"

"Trying to kick her way out," Dani confirmed. "At least that's what it feels like some days."

He lifted his gaze, revealing a savage exhilaration before he swiftly banked his expression to show only mild curiosity. "Does it hurt?" He spoke softly, his face close to hers, his mouth inches from her ear.

She moistened her lips, fighting emotions struggling for rebirth. "Not really. And any discomfort is worth it." She couldn't help smiling. "More than worth it."

"Are you...happy about the baby?"

"I've wanted one for a long time now. But Peter—" Nick stilled, and Dani realized that this wasn't the appropriate time to discuss the flaws in her former marriage. She shrugged awkwardly. "Yes, Nick. I'm very happy about the baby."

"You're just not happy I'm the father."

"I didn't say that!"

"You didn't have to. It doesn't take a genius to add up that particular equation."

"New Year's Eve was—"

"An aberration. Yes, so you've said."

His tone worried her, and she tried again. "The situation got out of hand." An understatement if ever there was one.

"It wasn't planned, that's for damned sure."

"Nor would I have chosen to get pregnant as a result of that night."

"But you did." The words hung between them, stark and incontrovertible.

"I want this baby," she said, repeating the only words that could possibly make a difference.

"You just don't want me." Slowly he removed his hands from her belly and rose. "You should have told me months ago. You had no right to keep your pregnancy from me."

Dani couldn't argue the point, much as she might want to. She sighed, inclining her head in acknowledgment. "I'm sorry. I guess I knew there would be consequences once you found out."

"But you weren't ready to face them." It wasn't a question.

"Not when those consequences involve marriage. No." She'd never willingly trust a man again—not with her heart and not with a commitment as sacred as marriage. Once had been quite enough.

"That's unfortunate. But it doesn't change my mind or my demands." Clearly, he didn't intend to give an inch. "Let's finish this, Dani. Do you agree to my terms or not?"

"Do I have any choice?"

"None."

"I could refuse to marry you."

"You won't."

She forced herself to regard him with as steady and impersonal a gaze as he so often used. "Yes, Nick. I can and I will."

He took a deep breath, as though bracing himself. "I'm afraid you're mistaken."

She hated when he looked like this, when he assumed the tightly focused stance and expression of a tiger moving in for the kill. She especially hated it when he'd focused that look on her. Because it meant she'd become his prey—and was about to lose. "And why am I mistaken?"

"Because all I have to do is pick up the phone. One call to your parents and the game would be over." Nick cocked his head, a weary smile tilting his mouth. "Checkmate, sweetheart."

Dani glared at him, disbelief warring with fury. "You'd call them?"

"In a heartbeat," he confirmed. "They must know by now that you're pregnant."

"It would have been a little difficult to keep it from them," she retorted dryly.

"Do they know I'm the father?"

"No."

A smile of satisfaction touched his mouth—a mouth she'd taken shameless delight in kissing on that one unforgettable night. "What do you suppose they'd do if I called and told them I was the father of your baby?"

"You mean after they picked themselves up off the floor?"

She failed to win a reaction. It would seem that Ice was once again in control of the situation. "Yes. After that."

"They'd be angry at you." She slanted him a quick, assessing glance. "Very angry."

"Right up until I explained that I didn't know about your pregnancy."

She grimaced. "Yeah. Right up until then."

"And when I told them I wanted to marry you?"

"They'd be thrilled," she admitted through gritted teeth.

"That's what I thought." He gave her a moment to consider her options before asking, "Ready to concede defeat?"

Dani silently stewed. Nick knew her parents far too well. He also knew, or suspected, the sort of grief she'd faced in the past six months, after she'd finally broken down and told them the news. Her relatives were a tight-knit bunch with a strong regard for the family unit. To her relief, they'd been thrilled about the baby. But they'd been terribly upset about her refusal to name—or marry—the father. And though they'd continued to offer their love and support, she knew her actions had hurt and disappointed them.

Still, she made Nick wait a full two minutes before giving in. "Marriage for one year. I'll continue on a limited basis with SSI. You'll buy out my share of the business at the end of that time. Agreed?"

"Agreed." He glanced at his watch. "I'll pick you up at nine tomorrow morning and we'll head over to the courthouse. I'll call and see if Judge Larson's available to perform the ceremony after we fill out the appropriate forms. With a bit of luck he'll cut through any red tape and have us married by noon."

"So quickly?"

"I don't think we have a lot of time to spare, do you?"

She hated that he was always right. Still, having agreed to marry him, she couldn't delay the inevitable much longer. Not if the baby was to bear his name. "I don't think there'll be time to arrange a church wedding."

"Do you mind?"

"Yes. But considering the circumstances..."

Nick inclined his head. "I assume you'll want your relatives there?"

She smiled wryly. "I don't think we could keep them away."

"Then it's settled."

Neither of them moved for a long moment. Then Dani rose, awkward in the fullness of her pregnancy but more awkward in the presence of the man soon to be her husband. "I'll show you out."

He didn't refuse, and she walked with him to the front entrance hall. "Take care of her, Gem," he requested as he opened the door. "And contact me if there's a problem."

"REQUEST ACKNOWLEDGED, MR. COLTER. HAVE A PLEASANT EVENING."

Dani frowned. "Now wait just a darned minute—"

"You're due any day, sweetheart," Nick interrupted in such a reasonable tone of voice she almost socked him in the jaw. "I just want to be sure there aren't any last minute complications. Gem will make certain of it."

"I don't like being spied on!"

"Gem isn't spying. She's protecting you. That's her job."

"That's her job for now," Dani muttered.

"It's her job until I tell her otherwise."

"Or until I get my hands on those override codes." Before he had a chance to confuse her with any more logic, she said, "You never told me why you came home early."

"Let's just say I had a feeling."

Dani lifted an eyebrow. "A feeling?" she asked politely. "You, Nick?" If she'd succeeded in annoying him, he didn't let on. Yeah, like that came as a surprise.

"Despite what you might think, I'm not a computer," he retorted with a calm she could only envy. "If New Year's Eve didn't drive that point home, I'll make sure I explain the difference—in full detail—sometime in the next year." And with that he stepped across the threshold.

As usual, he'd managed to get in the last word, which annoyed her no end. Knowing it was childish, she slammed the door in lieu of taxing her brain for an appropriate comeback. Then she thoroughly disgraced herself by sticking out her tongue. Gem chose that moment to have another hiccup in her voice modulator.

"Oh, shut up," Dani snapped.

"ERROR NUMBER EIGHT-OH-TWO AND FOUR-THIRTEEN. PLEASE FORMULATE REQUEST ACCORDING TO APPROPRIATE GUIDELINES. HAVE A GOOD DAY, MRS. SHERATON," came the smug response.

"Oh, I'll have a good day," Dani muttered as she waddled down the hallway. "Just as soon as I find a sledgehammer and some wire cutters. Then we'll see who has the last hiccup in whose voice modulator!"

Nick stood on the porch of Dani's home, his back to the closed door. The symbolism didn't escape him any more than the irony of his situation. Once more he found himself out in the cold. An image flashed through his mind, an image of a small, stoic boy.

He, too, stood alone, a closed door at his back, an empty parking lot stretching before him. He waited, just as he'd always waited. Behind him rose a factory-like schoolhouse, darkly outlined against a bleak, wintry sky. And as he waited a solitary snowflake drifted before his eyes, trembling within the grip of a chill wind. But he didn't move, refusing to acknowledge the cold or the rarity of snow in San Francisco or the lateness of the hour. Refused to allow the emotions battering at his soul to escape. Tears were useless, even if he'd still possessed the ability to cry. But he no longer could. They'd frozen long ago.

So instead he'd waited, just as he always waited.

The memory faded, and Nick lowered his head like a crazed bull preparing to charge. He clenched his jaw, and his hands collapsed into fists. Not again. Never again. He'd find a way inside, find the warmth he so desperately craved. No matter how long it took, he'd bask in the heat that was Dani.

*   *   *

"How are you feeling?"

Dani grimaced, shifting on the uncomfortable wooden bench outside the judge's chambers. Not that it did any good. No matter how often she changed her position or how hard she rubbed the muscles knotted at the base of her spine, she couldn't find relief. "Do you really want an answer to that question?"

"I wouldn't have asked if I didn't want to know."

"Okay, fine. There isn't an inch of me that isn't either swollen, sore or malfunctioning in painful and embarrassing ways."

Nick didn't laugh, as she half-expected. Nor did he offer useless platitudes. Instead he eased an arm around her and planted his fist in the small of her back. Very gently he applied pressure. "Better?"

She released her breath in a low moan of pleasure. "Where did you learn to do that?"

"Sheer instinct."

Instinct? Nick? She found that hard to imagine. He'd always been so methodical and disciplined. He definitely didn't strike her as someone who responded to impulse. No, that was her area of expertise. "There's something I've been meaning to discuss with you."

"More surprises?" Amusement tinged his voice. "Don't tell me we're going to have twins."

We! Her hands knotted in her lap as she considered the casually phrased connection. He was doing it again. He kept pushing the bond between them, reminding her that he had as much interest in the tiny life unfurling beneath her heart as did she. It shook her composure more than she cared to admit.

"No, I'm not having twins. At least, the doctor hasn't mentioned anything." This was so darned awkward. "It's about my relatives—"

"They're coming to the ceremony, right?"

"Yes. It's just… When I told them about the wedding they got the impression— They thought—" She cleared her throat. "They think we're getting married because we want to."

"I *do* want to."

"Yes, I know. You want to because of the baby. But they think it's because of me—because you're in love with me." She shot him a quick, nervous glance. "I didn't have the heart to tell them the truth."

He absorbed her comment without apparent concern. "How did they take the news?"

"They were thrilled," she told him honestly.

It surprised her that they'd accepted Nick with the same ease and enthusiasm as they had her impending marriage. Of course, her family had always liked him. She frowned. They'd liked and accepted him far better than they ever had Peter. But then, they knew the truth about her late husband—knew how lacking he'd been in both honor and emotional depth. And though she'd never had cause to question Nick's honor, he seemed incapable of any great feelings. In that single respect, both her husbands would prove the same.

"Did your parents ask why we'd waited so long?" Nick asked.

"Yes." The explanation had gotten just a wee bit sticky at that point. "I told them we'd delayed our decision until you returned from Europe because we both felt it was too soon after Peter's death to make a commitment. We wanted to make certain our feelings for each other wouldn't change."

"And they said?"

Her cheeks grew warm. "That if we were certain enough of our feelings to sleep together, we were certain enough to marry."

"I always did like your parents." She heard the trace

of amusement in the husky tones and shot him a dis-
gruntled frown. Not that he took any notice. "And the
baby? Did they wonder why I hadn't married you as
soon as I learned you were pregnant?"

She was afraid he'd ask that. "I told them you didn't
know about the baby until you returned from Europe,"
she admitted.

"That was brave of you."

"It was the truth." Honesty forced her to concede,
"At least that last part was."

"Which still leaves one intriguing question. Why *did*
you wait to tell me about the baby?"

She shrugged. "You were supposed to return in three
months, remember? I thought it would be better to break
the news to you in person."

"Liar. That might be what you've managed to tell
yourself all this time, but you didn't contact me for one
simple reason. You were afraid."

She set her chin. He could put her to the rack and she
still wouldn't admit the truth of that uncomfortable, al-
beit accurate, observation. She didn't dare look at him,
instead fixing her gaze on the opposite wall. "I wanted
to tell you in person, and I'm sticking with that story no
matter what. It wasn't my fault you extended your trip
to six months. Or nine. Good grief, Nick, the last time
we spoke you mentioned that you might stay over there
a full year."

"I'd have come back earlier if you'd told me. Hell,
I'd have been on the next plane without your telling me.
All you had to say was, 'Come home.'"

Home? She shied from the word. "Well, it wasn't
necessary, was it? You came back early, anyway." Her
back seized up again, and she grimaced, shifting on the
bench. Not that it did any good. Comfort was an experience she could only vaguely recall. "I couldn't believe

it when I opened the door and found you standing there.''

''I was a trifle taken aback, myself,'' he retorted dryly.

''You sure concealed it well.''

''Years of practice.''

That caught her attention, and this time she did look at him. ''Really? You've practiced hiding your emotions?'' Curiosity stirred. ''Why?''

''It seemed like a logical choice at the time.''

His idle tone didn't fool her. To her surprise, she was slowly learning to peek behind that nonchalant mask of his. It intrigued her, the mask he wore, practically begging that she uncover what he took such care to conceal. ''Something must have happened to prompt that sort of choice. What was it?''

''I realized the utter futility of emotional turmoil on one snowy December evening.''

''An epiphany, Nick? You?'' She tilted her head. ''And as a result you decided to follow in Mr. Spock's footsteps? Adopt the Vulcan philosophy of logic without emotion?''

He regarded her coolly. ''Let's just say I've never been offered an argument convincing enough to change my mind.''

''Something terrible must have happened for you to make such a radical decision.'' Her brows drew together, and a hint of distress edged her voice. ''What was it? Did someone hurt you?''

He never had the opportunity to respond—assuming he'd intended to. Just then Dani's parents descended on them, along with a multitude of brothers, sisters, offspring and various in-laws. As usual they were all laughing and talking at once.

''Congratulations!'' Dani's mother, Ruth, exclaimed as she approached. ''Now don't you worry about a thing, either of you, we have everything under control. And for heaven's sake, don't get up, Danielle! Nick, you make sure she sits right there until it's time for the ceremony." She gave her daughter a quick peck on the cheek before enfolding Nick in an exuberant hug.

Nick's bewilderment was a delight for Dani to see. It would appear he could stand a little more practice hiding his emotions. "What have you done, Mom?" she demanded, knowing her mother all too well. "What do you have under control?"

"Why, the wedding, of course." Ruth clapped her hands. "Come on, girls. Let's get this marriage off to a good start."

Dani's sisters crowded around the bench, each bearing a gift. Unexpected tears filled her eyes, a mixture of embarrassment and joy—embarrassment for allowing them to believe her marriage would be more that it was and joy because they cared and never hesitated to show it. "What is all this?"

"First is something old." Ruth grinned as a small package was offered. She dropped onto the bench beside her daughter. "Go on. Open it."

Dani ripped into the tiny gift box, tossing Nick a quick smile as he calmly collected the scraps of wrapping paper. Her breath escaped in a quick rush when she peeked inside. "Grandmother's locket. Oh, Mom. How can you bear to part with it?" Gently she released the catch and opened the scalloped fan folds. Inside was a photo of her and one of Nick.

He peered over her shoulder and lifted an eyebrow. "Where did you get that? Oh, of course. It's from the Christmas party two years ago. Clever."

"It took a bit of work, but we're a determined bunch." Ruth patted Dani's stomach. "Now, as soon as this little one makes an appearance you can add the baby's picture. Which leaves room for one more." She winked slyly. "Knowing how much Danielle loves children, I'm sure you'll have that locket filled in no time. After that, you're on your own."

A blush stained Dani's cheeks, but before she could comment another package was handed to her. "Something new?" she guessed, tugging at the pretty pink ribbon. She pulled off the lid of the box and froze. Inside she found a monogrammed ivory pillowcase, an elaborate silk N entwined around the D.

"We weren't sure what size sheets would be suitable," Ruth explained. "So we'll order the rest of the set as soon as you let us know. Do you like it?"

Dani drew a deep, steadying breath. Why hadn't she thought of this? Once she married Nick, her parents would expect them to live together like a real husband and wife, to share a house *and* a bed. She fought to keep her hand steady as she ran a finger over the delicate embroidery. "It's...it's beautiful. Thank you."

"As to the size," Nick added, much to her chagrin, "the bed's a California king."

Ruth chuckled. "I'll place the order the minute I get home."

"Now for something borrowed." Dani's oldest sister, Jamie, stepped forward. "I wore this at my wedding, if you'll remember." She handed over a large square box. "You admired it so much, I thought you'd like to wear it."

Dani removed layers of tissue from around the wide-brimmed hat her sister had worn in place of a veil. It was a dainty, feminine confection accented with lace and a huge satin bow and had set off her sister's dusky curls to perfection. No doubt it would do the same for her own. It was also the exact shade of the ivory gown she'd chosen to wear for the ceremony, and to everyone's delight, the lace on the hat closely matched the trim on her scalloped bodice.

"Thank you, Jamie." She fought to hang onto her smile, overwhelmed by her family's thoughtfulness. She hadn't expected it, and she should have. "What a wonderful gift."

Nick gently lifted the hat from the box and set it on her head. He tilted it slightly, so the wide brim dipped delicately over one eye. "You look beautiful," he informed her with a sincerity she couldn't mistake. "Perfect, in fact."

"Well, not quite perfect," her youngest sister chimed in. "She doesn't have my present yet."

Even Nick laughed at that.

"Let's see." Dani peeked out from under the hat. "We have something old and something new. And something borrowed. That leaves you with—"

"Something blue. You got it," Kendell said, holding out a narrow box.

"I'm almost afraid to open this one," Dani muttered, well aware of her sister's penchant for practical jokes. Sure enough, inside was a saucy black garter trimmed with a blue satin ribbon the exact shade of Nick's eyes.

"Let's see how it fits." With a teasing laugh, Kendell plucked the garter from the box and dropped to her knees in front of Dani.

"My job, I think," Nick claimed smoothly, easing Kendell to one side and taking her place.

Not giving Dani time to protest, he captured her ankle and removed her shoe. And then he looked at her with those incredible blue eyes, a hot challenge blazing from the bottomless depths. Carefully he tucked her foot into the crook of his thigh, daring her to so much as twitch. She drew a quick, nervous breath as ever so gently he slipped the garter over her instep and eased it upward.

At first his hands smoothed the narrow bones of her ankles. But then his fingers played along the sensitive skin, tapping out a primitive rhythm that fired her blood and filled her with sharp, sweet need. Part of her wanted to yank free of his hold, while another, more willful part wanted to slide into his embrace and relearn the steps to this particular dance. But with her entire family looking on, she knew she couldn't do either. So she sat in agony as, inch by torturous inch, he slid the garter along her stocking-clad leg. He continued past her calf to her knee, hesitating at the edge of her dress.

"That's good enough," she whispered urgently.

"Not even close," came his instant response.

Her family was no help whatsoever. Instead of taking her side, they egged him on, encouraging him to do his worst. A tiny smile tilted his mouth as he fixed her with a mocking look. Then his hands disappeared under the hem of her skirt as he tugged the garter ever upward. Finally he reached the border of her stockings. He mustn't have encountered this particular style before, because he took a moment to run the tip of his finger around the tight elastic edge. Searching for a nonexistent garter, she realized, fighting to contain a panic-induced laugh. He must not realize that garters and pregnancy didn't make for a successful match.

"What have we here?" he murmured.

Dani could see her sisters covering their mouths to hide their amusement. "I'm wearing thigh-highs," she whispered awkwardly. "They're trimmed with elastic so I don't need a garter. They're like knee-highs only... only higher."

"Very interesting. You'll have to show me."

"Not a chance!"

"But, sweetheart, I've never seen this type of stocking before." A wicked glitter ignited his gaze. "You, our baby and these stockings. Now there's something I'd give a fortune to see."

Oddly shaken, she protested, "Trust me, in this case ignorance truly is bliss. Besides, I'm in no condition to give you a peep show."

The humor faded from his eyes, and for an instant she could have sworn she saw a flicker of longing. "Your pregnancy makes you more beautiful than you can possibly imagine." He spoke with quiet conviction. "At least it does to me. And right now I can't think of anything I'd rather see than you in those stockings with our baby harbored safe within you. Well...nothing, except for my ring on your finger."

"Oh, Nick." His words totally overwhelmed her, and she could only stare at him, shaken by how swiftly he'd taken her from laughter to tears.

"Sorry to break up your little party, but they're ready for us," Kendell interrupted regretfully.

Nick released a gusty sigh. "I guess we'll have to save this for another day," he murmured.

With all too apparent reluctance, he slid his hands along a return path from thigh to knee to ankle before replacing her shoe and standing. He reached down, helping her gently from the bench, continuing to support her weight until he'd made certain her legs were steady. A good thing, too, considering how shaken she was from his foray beneath her skirt—and how cramped her muscles had become from sitting on the hard wooden bench for so long.

He stood to one side while her family trooped into the judge's chambers. At the doorway he hesitated, glancing up and down the hallway. She watched him curiously. "Nick?"

"I'm coming."

He waited another minute, checking the corridor a final time, and she frowned. What could he be looking for? Or rather, who? From something Peter had once said, she assumed Nick's parents were deceased. She also knew he'd been an only child, so it couldn't be family. Did he have other relatives, family he'd invited to their wedding and hoped would appear at the last minute?

"Who are you—" she began as he turned to join her.

One glimpse of his frozen expression killed the question. Winter had scoured all life from his face, and with the relentlessness of an arctic-driven nor'easter, it had swept straight to his soul. Dear heaven, what had caused such a reaction? she wondered helplessly. Only moments before he'd been filled with laughter and tender warmth, teasing her as easily as he had seduced her.

But in one brief instant, something had happened to this man, something that had stolen the emotions from his life and forced him inward. Something to do with what should have been in the hallway—and wasn't.

"Are you ready?" he asked.

His words might have been formed from bits of shattered ice, they sounded so brittle and sharp, filled with a terrible coldness.

"I'm ready," she whispered apprehensively. "But are you?"

He glanced at her, and it was all she could do to choke back a gasp. Dear heaven, his eyes were empty. So horribly empty. The blue irises had grown flat and steely, like a flame robbed of heat and light.

"There's no point in waiting. Is there?" And with that he slipped his hand beneath her elbow. "Let's go. We have a wedding to attend."

CHAPTER THREE

JUDGE LARSON proved to be an austere, keen-eyed man. He waited until everyone had filed into his spacious chambers before fixing Nick and Dani with a stern look. "Setting right a wrong, Nick?" he asked dryly.

Dani glanced uneasily at her future husband, wondering how he'd take the comment—especially considering his current mood. To her relief, he didn't appear offended. Instead he shrugged, saying, "I'm trying."

"And just in time, it would appear."

Dani winced, unwilling to allow Nick to take the blame for something she'd done—or rather, neglected to do. "The delay was my fault," she explained.

The judge inclined his head. "In that case, I'm relieved to see he finally convinced you to marry him. He's a fine man."

Her response didn't take a moment's consideration. "Yes, he is," she agreed.

Nick slipped an arm around her waist. "Henry, would you mind if Dani uses your chair during the ceremony? I don't think she should be on her feet any longer than necessary."

Only then did she realize that she'd been restlessly shifting her weight from one leg to the other in a futile effort to relieve the cramp centered in the small of her back. She gave Nick a smile of gratitude, fascinated when he returned it. Just that tiny twist of his lips altered his entire expression, easing the austere lines bracketing his mouth and thawing the iciness she'd considered part and parcel of his nature.

To her surprise, he dropped a possessive hand on her stomach. "I know I've pushed you into marriage," he said in an undertone. "But...are you sure this is what you want? There's still time to change your mind."

She shivered in response to the familiar words. They were identical to those he'd used before they'd made love, nine long months ago. She flashed on that particular night, the night that had created the baby pressed so tightly against his palm. He'd smiled then, too, with the same raw passion deepening his eyes to indigo. And her helpless response had been to tumble headlong into his arms and then into his bed.

"You sure pick your times," he informed her roughly. "You can't get that night out of your mind, either. Can you?"

He knew! Dammit, how could he? Was she that easy to read?

He'd kept his voice low, his words a mere rasp. But they abraded her emotions, leaving her feeling vulnerable and exposed. "If you don't want me to think about it, then don't smile like that! The only other time you did was—"

"Last New Year's Eve?" Another smile slashed across his mouth. But this one was harder, a fierce tilt to lips she'd once explored with wanton thoroughness. "Hell, sweetheart. Is that all it took? A smile? You should have told me years ago."

Her relatives' conversations ebbed and flowed around them, breaking in periodic waves of noisy chatter. Not that she had a clue what anyone said. Instead, her gaze fastened on Nick and she found herself cast into perilous blue waters with no option but to learn to swim or drown. In that moment, drowning seemed the safest option. She fought for air, bewildered to discover that something as simple as breathing had become impossible. "Nick, I don't think I can go through with this."

His smile turned tigerlike, the look he gave her filled with desperate hunger and savage need. "And I don't think I can let you go."

Fortunately, Judge Larson offered her his chair just then, allowing her to break eye contact and collapse into the thick leather upholstery. "Are we ready?"

Nick took a stance beside the chair. "Dani?"

It was up to her. She could tell her family she'd changed her mind, and they'd support her decision, regardless of their concern—and disappointment. Or she could give her baby a father. She glanced at the judge, saw the patience and understanding in his wise gaze. Taking a quick, shallow breath, she said, "I'm as ready as I'll ever be."

Nick captured her hand and gave it a gentle squeeze. "Go ahead, Henry."

And that's when it happened.

The nagging pain that had centered in her back throughout the day radiated outward in an intense, constricting band. The air whooshed from her lungs, and her hold on Nick became a death grip. Struggling to draw breath, she shot him a wide-eyed, panicked look.

Nick's comprehension was instantaneous.

"Henry?" He didn't raise his voice, but something in his tone succeeded in snagging the judge's full attention.

"You have something to say before we begin?"

"Just a request." He shot Henry a speaking look. "Dani and I have decided on the short version, if you don't mind."

Again comprehension dawned, this time in the judge's eyes.

Nick silently willed him not to let on to the rest of the gathering. If they discovered Dani had gone into labor, all hell would break loose, and this marriage would never become fact. Fortunately, Henry was no fool. Years on the bench had undoubtedly taught him to make swift—and accurate—assessments of people. The judge's gaze shifted from Ruth to the rest of Dani's relatives, and he gave an imperceptible nod.

"Actually, Nick, that was going to be my request," he commented easily. "I'm afraid my schedule's tight today, so if there aren't any objections we'll get the two of you married with the minimum of fuss."

"And not a minute too soon," said the irrepressible Kendell.

"It may not be a minute too soon, but it certainly is nine months too late," Ruth retorted in her most parental tone.

Dani's hand clenched in his again, and he looked down. Damn. If this was another contraction, they didn't have much time.

"Henry!" he barked.

The judge didn't require further prompting. "Dearly beloved," he began.

"Wait! The flowers. Who was supposed to bring the flowers?"

Nick didn't know which sister spoke, but he could have cheerfully strangled her. "I'll buy Dani a truckload the minute we're married. Keep going, Henry."

"We're gathered here today—"

"The child should have flowers." Austin, the father of the bride, spoke for the first time.

"Daddy, I don't need flowers." Dani caught her breath long enough to reply.

"I think I saw a street vendor selling them just outside the courthouse. It won't take long to run out there and buy a bunch."

"Fine." Nick dug his wallet from his back pocket and yanked out a wad of bills. "Who wants to volunteer?"

One of the nephews stepped forward, snatched the fistful of money and raced out the door. Judge Larson caught Nick's eye. Apparently, whatever the judge read there was more than sufficient to convince him to continue with the ceremony. "We're gathered here today to join this man and woman in matrimony."

"We're not going to wait for Christopher?" another sister complained. "I'm sure we can delay the ceremony for five minutes."

"Christopher will have to miss a word or two," Nick snapped. "His Honor has a tight schedule, don't you, Henry?"

Dani let out a soft gasp, and beads of sweat appeared on Judge Larson's forehead. "Very tight. In fact, I think we'll move straight to the really short version. Do you, Nicholas Colter, take Danielle Sheraton for your lawfully wedded wife?"

"This is rather unusual," Ruth murmured unhappily.

"I do," Nick snapped. "Keep going, Henry!"

"And do you—"

Dani groaned. "I do! I do!"

"Don't you even want to hear the words?" Austin demanded. "What sort of wedding is this, anyway?"

"I heard them last time, Daddy! The only thing that's changed since then is the man I'm saying them to."

"And thank heaven for that!" Ruth muttered.

"Do you have the ring, Nick?" Henry prompted.

"Right here." He yanked it off his pinkie, forced Dani's clenched fist open and shoved the diamond-studded band onto her finger. He didn't bother waiting for the judge this time. "You're mine now, Danielle Colter. Through the good times and the bad, in sickness, health and childbirth. Hell, sweetheart, you're just plain stuck with me.''

''You have such a way with words, Nick. I wish—'' She closed her eyes and winced.

''What do you wish, sweetheart?''

''That I had something to give you.''

''You will soon enough,'' he retorted roughly. ''Henry, are we through here?''

''Almost. If anyone has any reason these two should not be lawfully wed, let him speak now or forever hold his peace.'' He didn't wait for an objection. ''I now pronounce you man and wife. You may kiss the bride.''

Nick gave his wife a regretful look. ''Somehow, I doubt there's time for that.'' Grabbing the back of the chair, he spun it around and rolled it briskly toward the door. ''Clear a path, folks! Henry, think you can arrange for a police escort?''

The judge was already on the phone. ''I'll have them meet you by the front entrance. Don't panic, man. We'll get her to the hospital in time.''

''I never panic,'' Nick retorted. Although he'd like to. Right at this moment, he'd *kill* for that ability.

Ruth's mouth dropped open as understanding set in. She grabbed her husband's arm. ''Oh, my goodness. She's in labor. Danielle! You're in labor?''

''I thought it was a backache, but—'' She moaned softly.

''Oh, dear. Just like when I had Richey. By the time I realized I was in labor—'' Ruth's eyes widened. ''Unless you want her having that baby in the middle of the courthouse hallway, you'd better hurry, Nick!''

''Thanks, Ruth. I'll keep that in mind.''

He whisked the chair from the judge's chambers, through the outer office and into the hallway, grateful for the sturdy castors. It was almost as good as a wheelchair and a hell of a lot more comfortable. Dani clung to the armrest with one hand and anchored Jamie's hat with the other. "Hang on, sweetheart. The police will get us there in plenty of time."

He hoped.

If he hadn't been so worried about Dani, the reactions to the people they passed on their mad dash through the hallways would have been amusing. At one corner, a young woman lawyer struggling to get out of their path collided with a clerk. Her briefcase went in one direction, strewing the contents across the polished floor. His files flew skyward, raining papers on everyone within fifteen feet of the crash site.

"Maybe we should stop and help," Dani said uncertainly, shoving the wobbly hat brim from her eyes.

"I think we have more important matters to take care of," he managed to say with amazing restraint. "Besides, your relatives aren't far behind. They can lend a hand."

He risked a quick look over his shoulder, stifling a shout of laughter. Ruth and her mob had reached the disaster area. Far from helping, they roared straight through the middle of the confusion with all the speed and determination of a runaway train. Papers flew into the air again. The clerk toppled over in a dejected heap in the middle of the floor. The lawyer's briefcase careened off a wall, spilling the few bits and pieces she'd managed to collect. She let out a shriek of outrage, picked up her briefcase and hurled it after them. Everyone else stood around, laughing helplessly.

Finally reaching the front entrance of the courthouse, Nick plucked Dani out of the chair. "End of the road, sweetheart."

"Why? What's wrong?"

"Steps. We get to hike it from here. I don't see an ambulance yet, but the police have arrived."

She wrapped her arms around his neck and clung to him. Her taut belly was pushed tight against his chest, and he could feel her muscles contract with the force of her labor. He gritted his teeth and took the steps as quickly as safety would permit.

Dammit! He shouldn't have allowed the ceremony to continue. It had been pure selfishness on his part. He should have said to hell with the wedding and taken her straight to the hospital. If anything happened to their baby as a result of his negligence, he'd never forgive himself.

The officer stood by the squad car, and as they approached, he hastened to open the back door. Nick gently set Dani on her feet. She looked at him, her eyes huge and dark and slightly bewildered.

"Oh, dear," she whispered.

"What? What is it?" Please! Don't let her deliver their baby on the sidewalk, he prayed desperately. "What's wrong now?"

She glanced down. "I'm afraid I've sprung a leak."

It only took an instant to grasp what had happened. "Her water's just broken," Nick explained to the officer—a very young, fresh-scrubbed man who instantly turned pink around the ears. "We're going to need to get her to the hospital. Fast. Do you have a blanket we can use?"

Fortunately, the officer was intelligent and level-headed. He provided them with a blanket and waited until Nick had helped Dani into the back seat. Then he flipped on his emergency lights and took off, weaving through traffic with speed and skill as well as the liberal use of his siren. Apparently he wasn't any more interested in delivering a baby in the back of his squad car than Nick.

"The contractions are coming closer together," Dani announced nervously, before breaking off with a groan. Her hat trembled from the force of the contraction, dipping to caress her cheek as though in sympathy.

Nick locked his arms around her and cradled her close.

Hurry the hell up! he silently willed. As though intercepting his thoughts, the officer slammed his foot down on the gas pedal. "Five minutes, sweetheart. Just hang in there for five more minutes."

"I don't think I can wait that long! I need to push."

"No, you don't," he informed her grimly. "Not yet."

"Yes, I do!" She glared, her eyes glittering with ebony fire beneath a tumble of night-black curls. "It's my baby. I should know whether or not I need to—" She broke off, her hands clamping around his arms hard enough to cut the circulation.

"Don't push! You're supposed to—" What the hell was she supposed to do? He'd never felt so helpless and unprepared in his life.

"Breathe?" the officer offered helpfully.

Nick grasped the suggestion like a lifeline. "Yeah, breathe. You're supposed to breathe."

The instant she could speak again, she snapped, "I know that! I'm not a complete idiot. I did take lessons on childbirth and labor, you know."

He'd missed out on that, he realized with a pang. She'd attended those classes alone, or with someone else. He forced the thought from his mind, forced himself to concentrate on helping her. "Well, are you using them?"

"Yes, I'm using them! Haven't you been listening? I'm breathing loud enough to crack glass. Or did you think all these noises I've been making are how I—'' A muffled shriek caught in her throat.

Nick swore beneath his breath. "Pant. Try that, will you? I read somewhere panting's supposed to help."

"You want me to pant?" she demanded the instant she'd recovered her voice. "How 'bout if you try to pant while I lock your innards in a vise and squeeze hard enough to—'' She groaned.

He held her closer. "Trust me, honey. My innards are in a vise."

She buried her head against his shoulder, and her wedding hat tumbled to the seat in a forgotten heap of ivory lace and satin ribbons. "Why did you get me pregnant? All I wanted was to sleep with you, not have your baby."

The officer's ears turned pink again. "Did you now," Nick murmured. "I guess this time it turned out to be a package deal."

"I order à la carte and you give me a nine-course meal! You messed up, Colter."

Nick couldn't help himself. He smiled into the silky black curls clinging to her temple. "I'm really sorry," he said, careful to keep all hint of amusement from his voice. "If it makes you feel any better, I didn't plan for you to get pregnant."

"Well, it doesn't make me feel better. And you did a damn fine job for somebody without a plan." Another contraction hit, and air hissed between her gritted teeth. "You should have considered this possibility when you seduced me. Why didn't you? You're supposed to be the brains of the operation, not me."

"In case you didn't notice, my brain wasn't the one in charge that night," he muttered.

"Oh, great. You decide to cut loose for the first time in your blueprinted life and look what happens!"

The policeman glanced in the rearview mirror. "She must be in transition. That's the worst stage of labor right toward the end. Real painful. They always talk nasty when they're in transition. She doesn't really mean what she's saying."

"I do so mean it! We were supposed to have a one-night stand. And this is what I get for a single lousy night of incredible lovemaking."

That gave him pause. He lifted an eyebrow. "Incredible?"

"All right. Spectacular. Spectacular lovemaking. It still should have been more."

Trying to keep pace with her special form of logic took every brain cell he possessed. "What should have been more?"

"I should have gotten more than one night of spectacular out of all this agony. For what I'm going through I deserve months, maybe years worth of spectacular."

"I'll see what I can do next time."

"There's not going to be a next time!" She grabbed the lapels of his tux, practically ripping them free of the seams. "There is *never* going to be a next time. That was your one shot, and you hit the bull's-eye. Congratulations, darlin'."

"Definitely transition," the policeman muttered.

Nick eased perspiration-dampened curls from her forehead, not the least dismayed by her declaration. They were married now. He'd have a full year in which to change her mind. Plenty of opportunities to hit more bull's-eyes. "But it was one hell of a hit, wasn't it, sweetheart?"

In a heartbeat, anger slipped into sorrow. "I haven't even picked out names." Tears welled in her ink-dark eyes. "We'll have to call him 'Hey You.' He'll end up with a complex and hate us forever."

"If it's a boy we'll name him Austin, after your father. Or Richard, after your brother. If it's a girl..." He took a risk. A huge risk. "What do you think of Abigail?"

"Abigail?" She tried it out, whispering the name to herself. "I like it. It's sweet. A little old-fashioned, but pretty."

"So we're decided? If we have a girl, we'll call her Abigail. And if it's a boy—"

"What about your father? Don't you want to name a son after him?"

"I think Austin would appreciate it more."

Another contraction hit, one that took forever to pass. "Dear heaven, Nick. It hurts. Why does having a baby have to hurt so much?"

He hated being helpless, hated it more than anything in recent memory. "I'm sorry. If I could feel the pain for you, I would."

"It wouldn't work," she informed him sadly.

It was an irrational conversation—a totally ridiculous conversation—but it seemed to keep her mind off the baby's desperate rush to be born. "Why not?"

The police car screeched to a halt outside the emergency room entrance, and she glanced at him as the car door beside her flew open, her gaze filled with sorrow. "It wouldn't work because you can't feel."

Nick stood in the doorway of Dani's hospital room, holding a huge bouquet of flowers and feeling more awkward than he had in his entire life.

She looked up just then and smiled in delight. "Are those for me? You didn't have to do that."

He shrugged. "Christopher never did get back in time. And Austin was right. You deserve flowers on your wedding day." He walked in and handed her the arrange-

ment. The riot of colors stood out against the ivory and
lace of her Victorian-style nightgown, and the trail of
ribbons wrapping the bouquet cascaded off the bed. She
looked more like a bride than a woman who'd just given
birth. He plucked two blossoms from the display and
worked them into the curls tumbling down her back.
"You deserve more. A lot more. But this will have to
do for now."

"Thank you. They're beautiful." Dani nodded toward
a nearby bassinet. "And speaking of beautiful…"

Nick tore his gaze from his wife and studied his
daughter. Emotion choked him, and he found he couldn't
speak. He reached out, but hesitated at the last moment,
unable to bring himself to touch their daughter. She was
too perfect. The most perfect creature he'd ever seen.
Yesterday, he'd felt this little one kicking within her
mother's womb. And now he could count each finger
and toe. How the hell had that happened? It almost de-
fied comprehension.

"Do you want to hold her?" Dani asked softly.

"You don't mind?"

"Of course, I don't mind. You're her father."

Ever so gently, he slipped one hand beneath the
baby's back and head. Lord, she was tiny. So tiny she
practically fit within his palm. With exquisite care, he
eased her into the crook of his arm. She stared at him
with great, solemn eyes and blinked her lush lashes.
Then she heaved a mighty yawn for one so tiny and fell
instantly asleep. Just like that, she fell asleep. He
couldn't believe it.

"Abigail," he murmured, brushing a finger across the
downy crown of her auburn-tufted head. "Little
Abigail."

Dani eyed him curiously. "Is that a family name?"

"No. It's…just a name."

The nurse bustled in, wheeling a bassinet. "I'm afraid we're going to have to relieve you of this little lady. The doctor wants to give her a quick examination, and Momma here should get her rest." She didn't give Nick time to argue, but swept Abigail from his arms and placed her in the bassinet with the ease of long practice. Then she trundled the baby from the room.

Nick watched his daughter leave, amazed at how empty his arms felt. He'd held Abigail for only a few short minutes, and yet the attachment had been instant and irrevocable. He wanted her back. He wanted his child where he could see her, hear her, protect her. He took a step toward the doorway.

"It's been a wild day," Dani murmured.

He stopped in his tracks, torn between the demands of fatherhood and those of a husband. One look at his wife, and the husband within him won. Crossing to her side, he rested a hip on the edge of the bed. Dark smudges etched lilac semicircles beneath her eyes, and he traced them with his thumb. "In twenty-four short hours you've become a bride…and a mother. Quite a feat."

"I'm a fast worker," she said with a self-conscious smile.

She wanted to say something more, he could tell, but clearly had trouble summoning the words. Her hands closed around the sheet, knotting the crisp folds, and he knew it must be serious. Dread pooled in the pit of his stomach. Would she tell him to leave? Would she announce that their marriage had been a mistake? Did she plan to explain that now that Abigail bore his name, there was no point in waiting a year to divorce?

"What's wrong?" he prompted, careful to keep the question light. Emotionless. Calm. After all, he was a man who couldn't feel.

"I...I owe you an apology." She caught her lower lip between her teeth. "I said some terrible things to you on the way to the hospital. I don't know what got into me. Well, I do, but... I'm really sorry if I offended you. You didn't deserve that."

The sharp sting of relief brought a tight smile to his lips. "No apology necessary. You didn't offend me."

"I'm glad, because I don't think I could have managed Abigail's birth without you."

"Your family would have helped."

"It wouldn't have been the same."

No, it wouldn't. Certainly not for him. He'd held Dani in his arms that final half-hour of labor, soothing and encouraging as she'd fought to bring their daughter into the world. And she'd clung to him as confession after confession spilled from her lips. She'd wanted a baby. For years. She'd hoped for a boy. No, a girl. No, twins. Then, nothing mattered except the health of their child.

Next came regret. She'd wanted to call him. She'd picked up the phone hundreds of times, but had been too afraid. He'd have insisted on marriage, she explained.

"You know why."

"Yes. But I didn't want to get married again. Not until I found someone I could trust. Someone capable of loving me. I can't live like I did before, without any emotional support from my husband. I'm not a cactus."

A cactus? "No, you're not," he agreed. At that point, he'd have agreed with just about anything she'd said, no matter how illogical.

"I need fresh air and light and fertilizer. And I need water. Lots of it. I can't do all the gardening. Every once in a while, I need to be watered and weeded, too. Peter... He kept forgetting. He dried me up and choked me out."

Nick had understood then. And every word hammered

like a deathblow, because she was right. Peter, for all his charm and cleverness, had been totally self-absorbed. He'd been a taker, collecting what he considered his due as he skated through life. And though Nick had never skated through life, he was a taker, as well. He'd lived his life in solitude, cut off from people and emotions. Oh, he wanted what Dani offered, the promise lurking within those great, dark eyes. He wanted her warmth and caring and passion, just as he wanted the baby they'd created.

But the painful truth was…he had nothing to offer in exchange. He could take. But he couldn't give.

"The head is crowning," the doctor had announced at that point. "Watch in the mirror if you want to see the birth."

The next few minutes were the most miraculous of Nick's life. He continued to sit behind his wife, holding her tight against his chest, supporting her as she labored to deliver their child. He watched in amazement as the muscles of her womb rippled and contorted in this final, Herculean task.

And then it had happened. Their baby had slipped from one life into another, forced from the dark into the light of a new world.

"You have a daughter," the doctor had said with a pleased laugh.

"Abigail," Dani had whispered.

At that, the baby screwed up her little face and released the most delightful sound in the world—her first cry. A cry that completely drowned out Nick's quiet words of satisfaction. "My father rejoices."

"So you're not upset?"

Torn from his reverie, it took Nick a minute to switch gears. "No, Dani. You haven't said anything I didn't already know."

"I'm glad," she said simply.

"You need some rest. I'd better take off."

"Nick?" A curious flush tinted her cheeks. "Thank you for everything. The wedding and getting me to the hospital in time. And...and for being there when I needed you."

"You're welcome." He hesitated, unwilling to leave until he'd rectified one final omission. "I did forget something, though."

"What's that?"

"I never had an opportunity to kiss the bride."

He didn't wait for her reaction, afraid to chance a brush-off. Instead, he leaned forward and captured her lips. It was a gentle kiss, a whisper of sensation. He'd meant it to be brief. But the temptation to linger, to reacquaint himself with her mouth and taste was too much to resist. He deepened the joining, easing past the weak barrier of her closed lips to explore the delicate inner recesses. She sighed, her breath a warm balm, and he drank in her essence.

One night. One spectacular night, she'd called it. That's all they'd ever had. And yet every bittersweet moment of that night had become indelibly fixed in his memory. Slowly he released her, a single thought coalescing in his mind. *It wasn't enough.* It wasn't anywhere near enough. Dani had married him. She'd borne him a child. They were joined, joined through blood and circumstance. And he wasn't about to let her sever that connection. Not in a year.

Not ever.

"Are you coming back?" she asked sleepily.

"Oh, yeah, sweetheart. Count on it. I'm coming back."

Nick stalked to the bank of phones and snatched up the receiver. He punched in a set of numbers then hesitated, clicking the plunger to disconnect the call. Damn. His hands trembled like a child's. A frown creased his brow. This wouldn't do. Undoubtedly the excitement of Abigail's birth had caused it. Regardless of the reason, he needed to end it. He couldn't allow his emotions free rein. Not right now. It wasn't safe.

Control. He had to regain his control.

He closed his eyes, willing a particular scene to mind. He'd started picturing the scene as a child out of self-defense, discovering it helped him control his emotions and insulate himself from hurt. It came with the ease of long practice—an endless panorama of rolling plains, stretching clear to the horizons of his mind. A thick carpet of snow covered every inch of the frozen soil. The snow didn't glisten in the sun. There was no sun. No sound. No movement. No life. Instead a cast of bluish-gray stained the purity of the landscape as completely as it stained the sky above, muting all brilliance. The image held no pain, nor did it offer peace. It simply was. And there, in that barren wasteland, he kept his control.

Nick lifted the receiver with a rock-steady hand and punched in the phone number. It rang four times. It always rang four times. Then a woman's voice sounded in his ear. "We can't come to the phone. Leave a message. Please." The "please" came as an absentminded afterthought. An irritating, high-pitched beep shot through the phone line, followed by unnerving silence.

"It's Nick," he informed the machine. "Just thought you'd like to know... I'm a father. She's a beautiful little girl named Abigail. Six pounds, four ounces. Call me when you get the chance and I'll arrange a convenient time to visit. Oh, and—"

Another harsh beep assaulted his ear.

His jaw flexed. "The wedding was beautiful. Sorry you missed it."

Ever so gently he returned the receiver to its cradle. And then he walked away.

CHAPTER FOUR

DANI WAITED IMPATIENTLY for Nick to arrive at the hospital. She wanted to leave, to escape from those who liked to poke and prod and encroach on her precious moments with Abigail. But she couldn't go home without her husband's assistance, and unfortunately, he hadn't shown up yet.

"Be patient, Danielle. He'll be here soon," Ruth assured her.

"Maybe he's forgotten."

"Forgotten his wife and daughter in less than twenty-four hours? Nick?" Her mother grinned. "I don't think so."

"We could run you home," Kendell offered.

Before Dani had a chance to refuse, Ruth piped up.

"Absolutely not. That would be stealing a memory from Nick, and I won't allow it. He'll be here soon enough. Now the two of you show some patience."

To Dani's alarm, Nick chose that precise moment to arrive, appearing in the open doorway just in time to overhear her mother's comment. "Have I missed something?" he asked in a dangerous rumble.

To her utter amazement he wore lightweight denims topped with a cotton crew-neck shirt. The jeans had seen the inside of a washer so many times, they were bleached white in spots. And though loose, the thin material still managed to lovingly outline slim hips, a muscular backside and powerful thighs. As for the crew neck, it showed off his shoulders magnificently. Apparently Kendell thought so, as well.

"Wow! Talk about hiding your light beneath a bushel," she muttered. "I can't blame you for wanting to ring in the New Year with him. Yum!"

Dani silenced her younger sister with a glare, then turned her attention to her husband. Kendell was right. Far too much of Nick's light was on display. She drew her brows together. "It's Tuesday. Where's your suit?"

"Is that how he managed to hide those shoulders? Buried beneath pinstripes?" Kendell murmured. "That'll teach me to pay closer attention to the suits and ties I work with."

Nick folded his arms across a chest as magnificent as his shoulders and propped himself against the doorjamb. "Since I'm not going in to the office, I don't need a suit. And you still haven't told me what I missed. Who stole what memory?"

"You're taking a day off?" It was an astonishing concept.

"Yes." He tilted his head and held her with those incredible blue eyes, eyes that demanded an answer to his question.

An uncomfortable silence descended, one finally broken by Austin. "It's time we left," he announced, offering Nick his hand. "Your daughter is beautiful. Congratulations."

"It's a good thing you arrived when you did," Ruth added, giving her son-in-law a now-familiar hug. "You got here just in the nick of time."

"I seem to be making a habit of it."

"It's a good habit." She smiled gently. "Take care of your family."

For a brief instant, his grim expression eased. "You know I will."

Not that his good humor lasted. The minute her parents left—dragging a reluctant Kendell along behind—

he fixed his gaze on Dani. She wasn't sure which was worse, the remote logic with which he usually regarded those peopling his world, or this cold, jaded look he'd assumed.

"Well? Are you going to tell me?" he asked.

"It's just a phrase our family uses," she explained awkwardly. "Anytime we do something that should involve everyone else and choose to exclude them, Mom always says we stole a memory from them."

"And what memory were you going to steal from me?"

"I wasn't planning on stealing anything from you. Kendell offered to take me home—"

"Without me."

"Yes, without you. Before I could refuse, Mom stepped in."

She wasn't certain whether or not he believed her. Looking at it from his perspective, she could understand why. From the moment Abigail had been conceived, Dani had kept Nick in the dark. She'd stored up nine long months of memories, moments he'd never had an opportunity to share and could never reclaim. Worse, if she'd had her way, she'd have delivered their daughter without his presence or knowledge. For the first time, shame filled her.

Looking back, she realized she'd made a terrible mistake. She'd excluded him from experiences that were his by right. She frowned as she mulled that over. If their situation had been reversed—if he'd kept vital information from her, information that would have directly affected her life—she'd have been furious. She'd have been more than furious. She'd probably never have forgiven him.

And yet, instead of greeting her with fury, Nick had treated her with nothing but concern, respect and far more gentle caring than she deserved. True, he'd pushed her into marriage. But she could understand his reason for making such an outrageous demand, even if she didn't like it. The idea of his child bearing Peter's name must have been maddening, especially considering the animosity that had existed between the two men.

Dani bit down on her lip. "I really am sorry, Nick."

He didn't respond. Instead, he stepped into the room and crossed to the bassinet. He didn't hesitate. He reached down and stroked the smooth curve of Abigail's cheek. "I've never felt anything so soft," he murmured. "It's like touching rose petals."

"Nick—"

"Has the doctor approved your release?"

"Yes, but—"

"Then I'll have them bring in a wheelchair so we can go. I'm parked downstairs." He paused at the door, his back rigid. "And just so you know... I bought a car seat for Abigail. That's why I'm late."

Dani had thought she couldn't feel any worse. In one brief moment, Nick proved her wrong. She might be innocent on this occasion, but that didn't correct past mistakes. By the time he'd confirmed her release and returned with the wheelchair, she was ready to leave, Abigail clasped snug within her arms.

The ride home proved excruciating. Although solicitous and ever-helpful, Nick hardly uttered a word. He'd withdrawn to some secret place all his own, a place Dani couldn't follow. At long last they pulled up in front of her home—or rather, Peter's home, she realized uncomfortably.

Nick must have felt the same way. He eyed the stucco monstrosity with open displeasure. "The sooner you're out of here, the happier I'll be."

"Me, too. If it makes you feel any better, I'm hoping to find someplace smaller in the next year or so."

"That's not what I meant."

She'd suspected as much. "I realize it's too large," she continued doggedly. "But it'll do until after the divorce." There. She'd said it.

His mouth tightened. "No, it won't. I don't want you and Abigail staying here. I have a house that's more than adequate for the three of us."

"I'm not moving in with you."

"No?" He swiveled in his seat to face her. "How do you plan to explain your decision to Ruth and Austin?"

She set her jaw. "I'll think of something."

"They expect us to live together. Or have you forgotten that minor detail?"

He was thinking of those damned sheets, she could tell from his expression. "I haven't forgotten a thing!" She winced at the thoughtlessly sharp tone and cast a hasty look over her shoulder at Abigail. The baby slept peacefully in her car seat, oblivious to the discussion swirling around her innocent head. Deliberately lowering her voice, Dani said, "Living together isn't part of our deal, Nick. We agreed to a one-year marriage in exchange for my continued help at SSI. I did not agree to sleep with you."

"I'm renegotiating the terms."

"You can't!"

He lifted an eyebrow. "Oh, really? Try to stop me."

"That won't be a problem. It only takes one simple word. No."

To her utter astonishment, a smile cut across his face. "Yeah, right. I recall how much success you had using that one simple word last time."

"That's a rotten thing to say!" True, but rotten, nonetheless. "It was an accident. A mistake. A one-time event. It certainly isn't sufficient foundation for a marriage.''

"Isn't it?"

She recognized his intent the instant before he reached for her. "Please, don't," she half-moaned. "Not again."

His mouth was close, so damned close. "Why? Do you hate it so much?"

No, she didn't. And therein lay the problem. She liked everything about him. She liked his touch, his taste, his kisses.

Especially his kisses. But she also liked hot fudge on apple pie. That didn't mean it was good for her, particularly in large doses. But with Nick... One tiny slice wasn't enough. It didn't even come close to satisfying.

She shook her head in bewilderment. "Why me, Nick? Why not someone else?"

"Because no one else can keep me warm. And I want to be warm, sweetheart. I've waited a lifetime to be warm."

She didn't understand, at least not his words. The fervor of his kisses, the undisguised hunger—that made sense. There, and there alone, they were attuned. It wasn't love she felt. It couldn't be. Lust. Passion. Sexual appetite. All those things she could accept. But not love. She couldn't trust love, or the man offering it. Love meant she'd lose again. Love meant giving up her life. Love meant pain and coldness and disillusionment.

Love was unacceptable.

He closed that final inch separating them, sealing her lips with his, stopping her words as well as her thoughts. His kisses shouldn't get better. This desperate desire should ease with familiarity, not increase. And then sheer sensation took over.

How could she have forgotten how profoundly he affected her? Her lips parted, inviting the heat, welcoming the sweet invasion. He was a man of discipline, and yet the instant they touched, his control shattered. He demanded, then coaxed. Teased, then tempted. The movement of his mouth and tongue dictated a rhythm only he could sense. And yet, her body seemed to remember it, and she found herself following his lead, rejoicing in the raw power behind his primitive inner song.

His hands sank deep into her hair, tilting her head so he could fully explore her mouth. She clung to him while memories stormed her mind. She remembered that night, that incredible, unforgettable night. He'd made love to her on the floor in front of the hearth, and with each delicious thrust had forever imprinted himself on her heart and soul. Heat gathered in the pit of her stomach, and she almost groaned. She'd just had a baby. How could she possibly want him so soon after giving birth to Abigail?

That brought her up short. Oh, heaven help her. Abigail.

How could she have forgotten? With a quick twist, she pulled free of his hold, the sound of her breath in the enclosed car coming loud and frantic. Neither of them said anything for a long moment. Then he cupped her chin and forced her to meet his gaze.

"What you feel for me may not be a solid foundation for marriage. At least, not yet. But it's a start. Whether you like it or not, we're a family. This is my baby, too. And I fully intend to be a father to her."

"I wouldn't have it any other way."

"Yes, you would. But I'm giving you fair warning. I'm not going to allow it."

"What...what do you mean?"

"I mean that I don't intend to have any more memories stolen from me."

"I made a mistake." She confessed the painful truth.

"I should have told you I was pregnant. I'm sorry I didn't. More sorry than you'll ever know. But I can't handle this marriage. Not right now."

"And I can't let you go." They were the same words he'd spoken at their wedding ceremony, said in the same rough tone of voice. "You've given me a taste of heaven. Is it any wonder I don't want to leave?"

"I can't love someone like you." The words escaped of their own accord, a cry from the heart, an echo of a past hurt.

"Why?"

She flinched at the question. "I already told you. Because you're no safer to love than Peter." She couldn't survive another emotionless marriage. She couldn't!

"You're wrong, wife. You may not want me for a husband, but that's too damn bad. Because for the next year, you're stuck with me."

With that, he left the car. Circling to her side, he helped her out. Then he opened the rear door and extracted Abigail from the car seat. Cradling her against his shoulder, he inclined his head toward the front porch. "Let's go."

As much as Dani wanted to complain about his take-charge attitude, she didn't dare. At the door, she punched in her code three different times before Gem deigned to shut down the security system and allow them entry.

The instant they were inside, Nick handed over the baby. "System override," he snapped. "Colter zero-zero-one."

"WELCOME HOME, MR. COLTER," Gem responded.

"Request immediate system change. Do you have a copy of Dani's voice imprint in memory?"

"AFFIRMATIVE, MR. COLTER."

"All locks are to respond to her verbal request through level-two security. Is that clear?"

"AS THE PROVERBIAL CRYSTAL, MR. COLTER."

"What did you just do?" Dani demanded. "What did all that mean?"

"I don't want you fooling around with buttons and code numbers when you arrive home with the baby. From now on just announce yourself and ask Gem to open the door."

"Just like that? I say open sesame and everything unlocks?"

"Just like that. Although I'd leave out the 'sesame' part. Gem doesn't do humor."

"Wait just one darned minute. I want to make sure I understand this. I tell this hunk of miswired circuitry to let me in, and she does it. No alarms? No police? No buttons to push or numbers to remember?"

"Not a one."

"How long has she been able to do that?"

"From the beginning."

Anger stirred. "From the beginning. As in the very beginning? As in when Peter and I joined the firm?"

"Yes."

"Then why the *hell* have I had to remember all those damn numbers?"

"I thought you wanted Gem to operate that way."

It was the first time she'd ever seen Nick lie. He didn't even bother to hide it. He just stood there, stared right into her eyes and handed her a line of bull. "Oh! I could kill you for that! I've spent five miserable years trying to remember all those numbers you've given me and now you're standing here telling me it wasn't even necessary?"

"No."

"And the monthly code changes?" She fought to keep her voice down so she wouldn't frighten Abigail. But it wasn't easy. "That wasn't necessary, either?"

"It was necessary, though perhaps not as often as every month." She barely noticed when he slipped the baby from her trembling grasp. "Voice imprints would have been your best bet, since they're unique. Or you could have used a fingerprint analysis."

"I'm going to murder you. You did it on purpose, didn't you? You deliberately had us jumping through electronic hoops for your own amusement."

"Don't be ridiculous. That would require a sense of humor. And as you've taken great pains to point out, I don't have any more emotions than Gem. So how could I possibly derive any pleasure from your problems with my computer?"

"I don't believe this!"

"Believe it. Peter made absolutely no effort to understand the mechanics of operating Gem. He requested—No, check that. He *demanded* I install Gem in his house and *demanded* his own personal set of codes. So I gave him precisely that."

"And by giving it to Peter, you also gave it to me."

He smiled at her sarcasm. "Yes."

"You son of a—"

"Wrong. Peter was the SOB. He was arrogant and careless. He assumed his father's throne at SSI and expected everything to be handed to him as his right, instead of learning the business. His primary concern was the bottom line. How much money could he pull in as a partner? Not that he felt it necessary to work for that money." Nick's eyes darkened, filled with stormy threat. "He was a fool. He never bothered to ask about voice access or finger imprints, and yet, if he'd taken five minutes away from his golf lessons to read the sales literature, he'd have seen those options spelled out in black and white."

"I read the literature," she said indignantly. "I assumed those features weren't available with this model."

"Well, you were wrong. You could have come to me and asked, Dani. If either of you had done even that much, I'd have made the change."

She didn't doubt the truth of his statement. By forcing them to question Gem's abilities, and thereby admit their ignorance, he'd have made his point painfully—not to mention cleverly—clear.

The co-owners of SSI were clueless.

Peter wouldn't have been amused by the deception. As for her reaction… It stung. Though she was forced to admit if Nick had played this trick on anyone else, she'd have found it wickedly amusing.

Not that that let him off the hook. Before she could tell him as much, Abigail awoke. She opened her eyes and looked around. Then her tiny face screwed up and she let out a wail that would have done a two-year-old proud.

"This kid must be ninety percent lungs," Nick commented.

Dani took the baby. "Try half lungs and half stomach. She's probably hungry, so if you don't mind, I'll let you see yourself out." She made the request with amazing civility, considering she was still mad as hell. "I'm going to feed the baby."

At least she was going to try. She hadn't quite gotten the knack of this particular aspect of motherhood, not that she'd confess such a failing to her husband. Not after what he'd pulled. Clutching Abigail close, she stalked down the hallway toward the bedrooms.

"MR. COLTER?"

Nick sighed. "What is it, Gem?"

"IDENTIFY NOISE." There was a brief pause and then he heard a playback of Abigail's cry.

"That's my daughter. Her name's Abigail."

Again there was a pause, and Nick knew Gem was searching her computer banks for the term *daughter*. An instant later she came back online. "YOU HAVE PRODUCED A FEMALE OFFSPRING UNIT?"

"Yes, Gem. I have. And just so you know, Mrs. Sheraton is now Mrs. Colter. She's my wife and Abigail's mother."

"ONE MOMENT. ACCESSING. YOU HAVE FORMED A MARITAL BOND WITH MRS. SHERATON-COLTER?"

"It's just Mrs. Colter now, Gem. Feel free to wipe the name Sheraton from your memory banks." He took far too much pleasure in saying that. "And yes. I've formed a marital bond with her. At least, I'm trying."

"MRS. COLTER ASSISTED IN PRODUCING THE FEMALE OFFSPRING UNIT?"

"She gave birth to the baby, yes." He frowned as a sudden thought occurred. "Gem, set your systems to listen for that sound you recorded. If it continues for longer than three minutes, alert Dani."

"EXPLANATION?"

"That noise means the, er, female offspring unit needs immediate attention. Considering how huge this place is, Dani might not hear."

"AFFIRMATIVE, MR. COLTER."

"And Gem?" He hesitated, knowing his wife wouldn't like his next directive. But what the hell. She didn't like anything else he'd done these past five years. Why break a perfect record? "Activate the monitoring system. Contact me if anything unusual happens."

"DEFINE UNUSUAL."

"Unusual is an event that deviates from Dani's normal routine. The reports are to have security alert status one. Understood?"

"UNDERSTOOD."

"Reset system after I've left."

"AFFIRMATIVE. HAVE A GOOD DAY, MR. COLTER."

"Not bloody likely," he muttered.

And with that he forced himself to walk away from his brand-new family.

"MRS. COLTER?"

Dani came awake with a jerk, staring in bewilderment around the darkened room. "Gem? Is that you?"

"AFFIRMATIVE, MRS. COLTER."

"What is it? What's wrong?"

"FEMALE OFFSPRING UNIT ABIGAIL HAS BEEN EMITTING A HIGH-PITCHED NOISE FOR THREE POINT TWO MINUTES. I WAS INSTRUCTED TO ALERT YOU TO THAT FACT."

"Abigail's crying?"

"ONE MOMENT." An instant later the sound of infant wails filled the room. "PLEASE CONFIRM HIGH-PITCHED NOISE IS CRYING."

Dani was out of bed like a shot. "Confirmed!"

She raced through the open doorway between Abigail's bedroom and her own and lifted the baby from her crib, horrified that she hadn't heard the telltale squall. There was no mistaking this particular cry. Her daughter was hungry. Taking a seat in the rocker stationed nearby, Dani awkwardly unbuttoned the front of her nightgown.

This would be her fifth attempt to breast-feed the baby. One of those times had been in the hospital with a nurse in attendance giving her detailed instructions on what Dani had always assumed to be a simple—not to mention instinctive—procedure. Apparently, it wasn't any more simple or instinctive than programming Gem. She'd discovered that dismaying fact the three times she'd tried to nurse since returning home. Which reminded her...

"Gem, did you say you were instructed to alert me whenever Abigail cries?"

"AFFIRMATIVE. WHEN INFANT DAUGHTER UNIT EMITS HIGH-PITCHED NOISE FOR LONGER THAN THREE MINUTES, I'M INSTRUCTED TO INFORM YOU. LEVEL-ONE SECURITY ALERT."

"Nick! He told you to do that, didn't he?"

"AFFIRMATIVE."

As much as she wanted to countermand Nick's orders, she was sensible enough to realize his interference stemmed from concern. She let it go, focusing instead on her daughter's need for food. To her dismay, Abigail shook her head, refusing the proffered sustenance.

"Come on, sweetheart," Dani pleaded softly. "You have to eat."

Apparently, Abigail didn't agree. She cried—long, pitiful wails. Then she latched onto the nipple again, suckling hungrily for a few seconds, before letting go with a frustrated cry.

Dani rocked frantically, not knowing what to do. Why wouldn't the baby eat? What was wrong? Tears of despair filled her eyes, and she drew a weepy breath. She'd wanted a child so desperately, had always thought she'd prove to be a natural mother. And what could be more natural than breast-feeding her baby? Her breasts were achingly full, and yet as far as she could tell, no milk came in response to Abigail's sucking.

"MRS. COLTER?"

"Yes?" Her voice came out shrill and tearful.

"IS SOMETHING UNUSUAL IN PROGRESS?"

"What?"

"ARE YOU DEVIATING FROM YOUR NORMAL ROUTINE?"

"Yes, I'm deviating from my normal routine," Dani snapped, the tears spilling down her cheeks. "I'm a failure as a mother. Is that enough of a deviation for you?"

"AFFIRMATIVE."

"MR. COLTER?"

The light in Nick's bedroom turned on automatically, and he rolled over, instantly awake. "What is it, Gem?"

"SECURITY ALERT ONE. MRS. COLTER IS DEVIATING."

"What?"

"THERE IS A DEVIATION IN PROGRESS AT MRS. COLTER'S RESIDENCE."

"What's happening?"

"ONE MOMENT."

The sound of Abigail's cries filled the room, along with a second muffled sob. Dani! He rolled out of bed and into a pair of jeans folded neatly at the ready. "Relay picture. Now."

The TV screen flickered to life. At Nick's brusque command, the camera zeroed in on Dani sitting in a rocking chair with the baby clasped close to her breast. For some reason the pair of them were crying for all they were worth. He snatched his keys off the dresser and was out the door in two seconds flat.

CHAPTER FIVE

"DANI?"

She swiveled toward the bedroom door, her breath catching mid-sob. Nick stood there, clad in a pair of jeans—and nothing else. "Nick? What are you doing here?"

"Gem told me you were in trouble. What's wrong? What happened? Why are you crying?"

Distracted, she glanced at the baby. "It's Abigail. She won't eat."

"Why not?"

"I don't know! If I did I wouldn't be crying."

"Okay, okay." He hunkered down beside her and lifted Abigail into his arms. "What's wrong, sweet pea? You sound pretty hungry for someone who won't eat."

"It's my fault! I don't think she's getting any milk."

"Didn't the nurse say it needed to come in or something?"

"Come in, let down, who knows? But it's not working. I think it must be stuck." She drew a shaky breath. "Maybe I have a clogged pipe."

"I seem to remember her saying you had to be relaxed for everything to work properly." He gave a wry smile. "You don't look very relaxed."

"I see your powers of observation are as keen as ever." He didn't react to her waspish comment, just continued to regard her with a calm, reassuring gaze. "I'm sorry," she whispered, overcome with remorse. "I'm trying so hard to get this right. And it's just not working."

."Didn't the nurse suggest you take a warm shower the first few times?"

"I'd forgotten," Dani confessed.

"Okay. You hop in the shower and I'll hang on to the little squeaker, here. Then climb into bed, and we'll give it a try there. That should be a little more relaxing, don't you think?"

She didn't need a second bidding. She was willing to try anything. Closeting herself in the bathroom, she stripped off her nightgown and adjusted the spray to a warm, relaxing temperature. Her breasts felt painfully full and burning hot. Considering her condition, nursing should be a snap. Tears welled in her eyes. Maybe she was an exception. Maybe she'd been plumbed wrong. She allowed herself a quick cry, then, after a few minutes, shut off the water. The towel hurt, abrading her sensitive skin, but she gritted her teeth and persevered. Slipping on her nightgown, she walked into the bedroom and stopped in her tracks.

Nick occupied the middle of her bed, and he wasn't alone.

Looking as though he'd been born to the role of fatherhood, he held Abigail in the crook of his arm, the knuckle of his pinkie lodged firmly in the baby's sucking mouth. He'd piled a half dozen pillows behind him, and when he spotted her, he spread his jeans-clad legs, patting the narrow space between them.

"Ready to give it another try?"

She moistened her lips apprehensively. "What do you think you're doing?"

"Making room for you."

"I mean... Why are you here? In my bed?"

"Come on, Dani. You need help, and I'm the only one available. Sit with me, and let's see if we can't figure this out together."

She didn't want to join him. She *really* didn't want to. It was too intimate, too suggestive—too reminiscent of nine months ago. "Nick—"

"We weren't here that night, remember? We were at my place."

"Stop reading my mind!" She caught her lip between her teeth. "How do you always know?"

He shrugged. "I'm psychic."

"I'm serious. How do you know?"

"You want the truth?"

"Please."

"You blush."

She gave it a moment's thought. "That's it? I blush?"

His mouth twisted. "And you do this…this thing with your eyes."

"What thing?"

"Come on, wife. You're wasting time. Get over here."

Wife. Almost, she retreated. But then Abigail began to fuss, taking the choice out of Dani's hands. With a tiny groan, she surrendered to the inevitable. Clambering onto the bed, she slid between Nick's legs, gingerly wriggled her backside into the narrow gap between his thighs.

He hadn't left much room, and she suspected it was deliberate. Correction. She *knew* it was deliberate. He cradled Abigail in his hands, then passed her to Dani. Then he pulled them both into his arms. She could feel his heat through the thin cotton of her nightgown, feel it burning a path the full length of her spine. Worse still was the subtle play of muscle and sinew shifting across her back as he settled against the pillows. How was she supposed to relax when he sat behind her half-naked? Couldn't he have bothered to drag on a shirt before he came over? It would have taken...what? An extra two seconds?

She closed her eyes. No, Nick wouldn't have wasted even that much time. She'd needed him, and he'd come running. She drew an uneven breath, praying he didn't sense her distress. Why did he have to be so generous and committed? Why couldn't he be more like Peter and play his assigned role of selfish bastard? Neither of them believed in love. How could they, when they were incapable of feeling? Perhaps if Nick would admit as much she could erase him from her life—and even more importantly from her memories.

Her memories! Dear heaven, how they haunted her. New Year's Eve had been a dream, and a bittersweet one, at that. The Nick she'd fallen in love with on that single surreal night didn't exist. It was too dangerous to think he might. Too risky. It was far better to believe that she'd created the ultimate fantasy lover, given him the characteristics she'd always wanted in a man. She'd pretended he was strong and yet tender. Invented the desperate passion and hunger with which he'd taken her. Only imagined the look in those fierce blue eyes, the look that said he'd been waiting a lifetime to make her his.

It wasn't real.

She had to face the painful truth—no matter how much she might want it otherwise, her husband couldn't fulfill her needs. He'd kissed her after picking her up from the hospital, knowing full well what her reaction would be, knowing it would be the easiest way to get what he wanted—his daughter. He was as logical and emotionless as the computer program he'd invented, and just as incapable of experiencing love. And though she knew his concern for his brand-new family was genuine, that he truly wanted to be a good father to his daughter and a good husband to her, she couldn't allow him to drag her into the barren wasteland of his life. Peter had almost destroyed her with his deceit and emotional capriciousness. She wouldn't give Nick Colter the opportunity to finish the job. She wouldn't let him freeze the life from what little remained of her heart and soul.

His jaw brushed the side of her head. "Go ahead, sweetheart. Give it a try."

Painfully self-conscious, Dani opened the front of her nightgown and put Abigail to her breast again. Not that it did any good. The baby instantly began to fuss. "I told you! I can't do this."

"Sure you can. You're just nervous. The nurse said that was normal in first-time mothers. Close your eyes."

"Why?"

"Not why. Just do it. Close them."

It was easier to give in. "Okay, they're closed."

"I've been thinking about this problem."

"Logically, no doubt."

She felt him shrug. "Is there any other way? The point is, it occurred to me that the first time you use a pump, it has to be primed."

"How do you prime a pump?"

"Well, normally you back feed water down the line to force out the air. Once the air bubble is worked free, bingo. The water starts flowing."

Her eyes flew open. "Um, Nick? I don't think you can back feed this particular pump. Let me rephrase that. You're *not* going to back feed this particular one."

He chuckled, the sound rumbling through her. "Don't panic. I thought we'd use a slightly different sort of priming method."

"Like what?" she asked warily.

"Well, the reason we can't prime this pump is that tension has gotten your lines in a kink. Water—or rather, milk—can't flow down a kinked line.'' He cupped her shoulders, massaging gently. "Let's see if this won't help.''

It wouldn't. No way, no how. If she had the nerve, she'd tell him as much. How could she possibly unkink with his hands all over her. "Nick—''

"Shh. Keep your eyes closed and let me loosen up these muscles. Gem, how about playing Kenny G? Keep it low, please.''

"AFFIRMATIVE, MR. COLTER.''

Instantly the clear, melodic sound of a soprano sax filled the room. Nick rubbed her shoulders and neck in rhythm to the music, his thumbs finding the various knots in her muscles and working them free. After a few minutes, Dani stopped resisting and allowed his strong hands to work their magic. Lord, she was tired. So much had happened in the past few days, not the least of which was the newborn daughter she held clasped to her breast and the newlywed husband wrapped all around her.

"Let go, sweetheart.'' His voice was low and rough, just inches from her ear. "Lean against me. I'll keep you safe.''

Without thought, she relaxed into his embrace. Abigail whimpered and latched onto the nipple once again. Dani froze as a tiny tingle rippled through her breast, an odd sort of surge she'd never experienced before. The baby began sucking avidly.

"Oh!'' Dani blinked in astonishment.

"Is that a good oh?''

"It's a very good oh.''

Nick's nimble fingers stilled. "Did your milk come in?''

"That's an understatement.'' She peeked at the front of her soaked nightgown. It would appear the on switch for this particular pump controlled both spigots. How odd. She'd never realized. "I think your priming method is an unqualified success. I'm leaking all over the place."

"Don't worry about it. Everything will wash."

Pleasurable sounds filled the room—Abigail's wet suckling providing an interesting accompaniment to Kenny G's poignant wail. Dani burrowed into Nick's embrace and closed her eyes again, unbelievably content now that this first roadblock had been successfully hurdled. His arms encircled her and Abigail, ringing them in warmth and security.

She turned her head, and her cheek grazed the fine brown hair dusting his chest. Once upon a lifetime ago, she'd slept, pillowed in just that spot. Her dreams had been sweet, and enchantment had filled the air. "How did you know I needed help?" she asked, more to distract herself than because she really wanted to know.

"Gem alerted me."

He caught her by surprise with that one. "I didn't realize the two houses were linked."

"They weren't until last night."

Dani opened her eyes. "You put us on the same system?"

"The minute Abigail was born."

The minute... "How long did that take?"

He yawned. "Most of the night."

"And then you went out and picked up a car seat."

"First the car seat, then my family."

He spoke without inflection. Still, she sensed the steely undercurrent beneath his words. From the minute he'd arrived on her doorstep and discovered her pregnancy, he'd done everything within his power to take care of her and Abigail, to push his way into her life and that of his daughter. Every step of the way, he'd met her fierce resistance with an equally fierce determination. Undoubtedly, his goal was to make himself indispensable. And although she might find his take-charge attitude overwhelming at times, even presumptuous, she'd never once doubted the sincerity of his motives.

He just wanted what she couldn't give.

"How did Gem know to contact you tonight?"

"I told her to alert me if anything unusual happened."

She recalled Gem's odd questions. "You mean, if I deviated from my normal routine?"

"Something like that." He tucked a strand of dark hair behind her ear. "Does it bother you?"

She decided to answer honestly. "A little."

"Perhaps you should consider this. Since you won't move in with me, I need to know you and Abigail are safe. Gem can make certain of that. Anytime you want me, just tell Gem, and she'll track me down."

Dani lifted the baby to her shoulder and rubbed the tiny back until she'd coaxed free a bubbly burp. "You always have to be in control, don't you, Nick?"

"If taking care of you and Abigail means being in control, then yes, I do. You're my family now. Don't ask me to ignore that. I can't do it."

"It's not just us. It's the business, your personal life, even Gem. What do you suppose would happen if you let go a little?"

"I know what *did* happen the one time I lost control. You became pregnant, and my daughter was almost given another man's name." He didn't wait for her response—assuming she could have come up with one. "Now you tell me something. What would you have done if I hadn't come over tonight?"

"I'm not sure," she admitted. "I guess I'd have called my mother or the hospital and asked their advice. And if I still hadn't been successful breast-feeding Abbey, I'd have given her some formula.''

''And you'd have missed out on nursing. Isn't having that experience worth sacrificing a little of your privacy?''

''I suppose so.'' She sighed. ''All right, yes. I'm glad you came.''

''If you moved in with me, I wouldn't have to drive over in the middle of the night the next time there's a problem.''

''Don't push your luck, Nick. You've gained enough ground for one evening. Let it go.''

''Fair enough. I'll drop it.'' His voice was level, but she heard the subtle warning in his tone. ''For now.''

Gently, he released her. She couldn't help but stare as he stood and stretched, every inch the picture of raw masculine grace and power. His blond hair was rumpled, a fascinating jumble of dark and light streaks, and it pleased her to discover that disorder had managed to creep into this one tiny part of his life. Of course, she couldn't say the same about the rest of him. His body had been beautifully designed and crafted, his shoulders every bit as broad as she remembered, the skin still a deep golden hue. The brown hair matting his chest formed an inverted pyramid, vanishing into his low-slung jeans. She followed the line and then glanced down the length of his denim-clad legs. Sudden amusement helped ease the sharp pang of desire.

''Left in a hurry, didn't you?'' she commented.

''What?''

''To come over here. You left in a hurry.''

''I floored it. Why?''

''You forgot your shoes.''

''And my shirt. And my wallet.''

''That's not like you.''

He lifted an eyebrow. "Really? How would you know?"

"Five years of observation have taught me a few things about you."

He shook his head. "I may have been your business partner for all those years. I may be your husband now. And you may have pigeonholed me as a result. But, sweetheart, you don't know me."

She shivered at the arctic turn his voice had taken. "What don't I know, Nick? Explain it."

"Move in with me, and you'll learn soon enough."

For the first time, she sensed danger. Sensed it with an instinct she'd never known existed. It stirred within her, springing to life as surely as the instinct to subdue and conquer stirred within Nick. Her mouth went dry, while an unnerving combination of fear and excitement unfurled deep within her loins. His nostrils flared as though testing the air, and a strange certainty filled her. He was drinking in the scent of her, tuning his senses to her unique essence. Heaven help her! He was imprinting her in his memory for some time in the future when he could act on the helpless desire she'd unwittingly revealed.

"Abbey's fallen asleep." Her comment escaped in a nervous rush.

His smile flashed within the soft light of the bedroom, filled with hungry knowledge. "Why don't I change the little squeaker and put her to bed? You need to get some rest."

She didn't object when he slipped the baby from her arms—until she realized how exposed it left her. Her nightgown gaped in the front. And where it didn't gape, the thin cotton clung, damp from excess milk. Nick didn't look away, but stared with undisguised fascination. Her appearance had changed over the past nine months, motherhood ripening her curves so she could nourish his child, altering the shape and texture and color of her breasts. Even relieved of milk, they were larger than before. Dark blue veins showed through the paleness of her skin, and the nipples had enlarged, darkening to dusk.

"I've never seen— I never realized—" He broke off, dragging air into his lungs. "You look beautiful, sweetheart."

She gathered the edges of her nightgown and pulled them closed. What sort of response should she offer? Somehow saying thank-you didn't strike her as appropriate. Nor was this a situation her mother had covered in any of their various conversations about love and marriage. "Are you...are you leaving after you put Abbey down?" she asked awkwardly.

"I'm sure as hell not staying here."

She should let it go. She really should. But she couldn't. She was driven to ask the question she'd be better off avoiding. "Why?"

"I won't sleep in another man's bed."

Her mouth tightened. "That wasn't an invitation. And just as a matter of record, we never shared this bed."

"But you shared this room." He didn't bother to conceal his distaste. "You shared this house."

"Is that so bad?" she asked in distress. "I can't pretend our marriage never happened."

"I'm not asking you to." He cradled Abigail against his shoulder with a naturalness surprising in a day-old father. "But I won't take his place."

"You can never do that," she stated. And it was true.

Peter had been a boy, playing at life. Nick was a man, doing a man's job.

He studied her for a long minute. "I'm sorry. I know you must miss him."

It was a generous comment, especially considering how he'd felt about Peter. But the sad truth was, she didn't miss her late husband in the least. She regretted his death, true. She just didn't miss him. Not at all. "I have no complaints."

He dismissed the subject by turning away. "Change your nightgown and try to get some sleep, sweetheart. I suspect our daughter will want another feeding before long. Contact me if you need help again."

"I will." He started for the door and she called to him, allowing impulse to override caution. "Nick?"

He glanced over his shoulder. "Yes?"

"Just so you know. You've given me far more than Peter ever did." At his questioning look, she nodded toward their daughter. "I've wanted a baby for years. I was desperate to have one. Peter didn't give me Abigail. In fact, he couldn't, even if he'd wanted to. You did that all on your own."

"What do you mean, couldn't?"

"Peter was sterile."

Shock glittered briefly in Nick's eyes. "Was he?" A curious expression sparked in his gaze. "How very interesting."

And with that enigmatic comment, he left the room.

Nick settled Abigail in her crib and stood for a long moment studying his daughter. "Good night, sweet pea," he murmured, spinning the nursery rhyme mobile hanging over one end of the crib.

"MR. COLTER?"

He smiled at the computer's attempt to imitate his whisper. "Yes, Gem. What is it?"

"EXPLAIN THE CORRELATION BETWEEN FEMALE OFFSPRING UNIT, KENNY G AND SUCCESSFUL ATTEMPT AT NOURISHMENT."

"Kenny G helped Dani relax enough to feed the baby."

"EARLIER ATTEMPTS WERE NOT SUCCESSFUL?"

"No, Gem. They weren't."

"MUSIC IS NECESSARY FOR SUCCESSFUL NOURISHMENT TECHNIQUE?"

"It would appear so." Silence reigned, and he gave Abigail a final lingering look. "Don't worry, little one. It won't be long now. I promise."

Dani gritted her teeth. "I don't care what Mr. Colter told you. Mrs. Colter has been listening to nothing but Kenny G for the past two weeks. Now turn it *off*!"

"KENNY G IS REQUIRED FOR SUCCESSFUL ATTEMPT TO NOURISH FEMALE OFFSPRING UNIT."

"Kenny G is no longer necessary for successful attempt to nourish female offspring unit. In fact, if you don't shut it off right now, the attempt to nourish female offspring unit will fail. Do you understand me, you pathetic heap of miswired circuitry?"

"PLEASE USE PROPER FORM OF ADDRESS WHEN MAKING A REQUEST."

"Gem! Turn off that music." When obedience wasn't immediate, she snapped. "Security one alert. Inform Mr. Colter that I'm deviating from my usual routine."

"PLEASE CONFIRM. SECURITY ONE ALERT IN PROGRESS?"

"Confirmed!"

Fifteen seconds later, the phone rang. It was Nick. "I'm on my way. What's wrong?"

"Tell Gem to turn off Kenny G."

"What?"

"You heard me! I don't care what else she plays, but

if I hear another saxophone, I'm going to take a hatchet to the wall and start chopping up electrical wires until I've managed to disconnect her.''

"Gem!"

Instantly Mozart blasted through the speakers. With a sigh, Dani set the rocking chair in motion. "Thank you," she said, dropping the telephone receiver into its cradle. Apparently, there was more than one way to skin a computer.

Nick stood in front of the blank TV screen, struggling to do the right thing. To make the moral choice. To take the higher road. He managed for all of thirty seconds.

"Monitor on," he rasped, giving in to the baser side of his nature.

The picture blossomed to life. Dani sat in the rocking chair in Abigail's room, nursing their three-week-old daughter. The camera was a good one, giving perfect color and sharp detail. It zoomed in. From the creamy, blue-veined skin of his wife's breast to the tiny fingers splayed across that plump curve, the image came through in full detail. Abigail gazed at her mother, sucking contentedly, a tiny line of milk leaking from the corner of her puckered mouth. Every few minutes, she'd wave her hand. But always it returned to pat the source of her nourishment.

His reaction to the scene was instant and unmistakable.

"Sound," he ordered in a voice he barely recognized as his own.

"MR. COLTER?"

"I said sound, Gem."

"IS SOMETHING UNUSUAL HAPPENING?"

He grimaced. "Yeah. You might say that."

"YOU ARE DEVIATING FROM YOUR NORMAL ROUTINE?"

"Yes, Gem. I'm deviating something fierce."

"UNDERSTOOD."

"Gem? The sound, dammit!"

For some reason she didn't respond. On the screen, Dani's head jerked up, and he realized she was talking. He frowned, thoroughly irritated. If Gem had done as he'd requested, he'd be able to hear what his wife said. An instant later, she stood and hurried from the room.

"Just great. Where the hell is she—" The phone beside him shrilled, and he picked it up, swearing beneath his breath. "Colter," he bit out. "What?"

"Nick? It's Dani. Is everything all right?"

Caught off guard, it took him a moment to respond. "Fine. Why?"

"Gem told me you were deviating. What's happened? What's wrong?"

He closed his eyes. "Nothing's wrong."

"Then why are you deviating?"

"I am *not* deviating."

"Gem said—"

"When did you start listening to Gem?"

"Starting right now. I'm coming over."

Anger flashed. "If you show up here, it's to stay. You got that?"

A sigh slipped through the phone lines, and he felt as though she'd touched him, stroked him, wound herself around and through him. His hand clenched, and he fought the desire battling for release. He burned for her, burned to turn that sigh to a moan, to reacquaint himself with every precious inch of her.

They'd made love twice the night Abigail was conceived, once in haste and desperation. But the second time... Heaven help him. It haunted his dreams still.

That second time had been unreal. He'd never had a woman so open or so honest, a woman who'd given her body with such unstinting joy. More, her heart and soul had been passed into his keeping. He held them still. Unfortunately, she was off-limits.

At least, for now.

"Please, Nick," she whispered. "Let me help."

"Not this time. Any deviations are all my own."

"It's a one-way street, is that it? You come running the minute Abbey or I need help, but we're not allowed to do the same?"

"Marriage is a two-way street, wife. Come if that's what you want." He paused a beat. "But once you do, you're not leaving."

"I can't do that," she retorted in a low tone. He could see on the television screen that she practically dragged the words free, see the pain they caused her. "I won't live another empty marriage."

"It won't be empty, Dani."

"Don't you understand? You're as incapable of emotion as Peter. He paddled around in the shallow end of life. It never occurred to him that there might be deeper, richer waters to explore. You're aware of those depths, I'll give you that. But you—"

He fought past the knot in his throat. "Go on."

"You avoid the deep end, too."

How little she knew. "What's your point?"

"You've buried your emotions so deep and for so long, I'm not even sure you'd recognize one if it walked up and socked you in the jaw."

His hands clenched. Once. Twice. A third time. Finally he gained enough control to ask, "Finish it, Dani. Say what you have to say."

"I won't have Abigail live that sort of barren existence. I grew up surrounded by love and laughter and warmth. And I've—'' Her voice broke. He watched her image on the monitor as she struggled for control, clasping the baby close as though to draw sustenance from her daughter's life force. ''I've lived in the cold for so long. I can't go back to that. It would kill me.''

Nick closed his eyes, unable to utter a single word. Control. He needed absolute control. It wasn't easy to achieve. His mouth twisted. Fortunately, practice made perfect. At long last, he opened his eyes. ''I understand,'' he replied calmly. ''I wouldn't want to do anything to hurt you or Abigail.''

''Nick—''

''Don't worry, Dani. I'm fine. We'll speak tomorrow.''

''Wait, Nick—''

Ever so gently, he returned the receiver to its cradle. ''Image off,'' he whispered.

Instantly, the screen went dark.

CHAPTER SIX

Dani sat in Nick's office, wishing she had the nerve to discuss the real reason she'd come instead of talking about SSI's financial situation.

"Are you listening, Dani? This is serious."

"I'm listening. I just don't understand." She frowned, putting aside her concerns about the previous evening's conversation. They could discuss that later. Even turning her full attention to their current discussion, though, didn't make the information any more comprehensible. "How could we be in financial difficulties? The last statement you gave me says just the reverse."

He focused on the papers spread across his desk. It struck her as odd that he avoided looking at her. She'd never seen Nick do that before. "We have more competition now," he finally said. "And without Peter keeping an eye on our domestic concerns while I was overseas, we have some catch-up work to do."

Her frown deepened. Peter's contribution had never been all that much. He'd specialized in sales. Even in that arena, he'd put in as little time as he could manage. So why would his loss cause such difficulties, especially when Nick had a whole army of salesmen and marketing types for that very purpose?

"I still don't understand."

"Then let me keep it simple. Our domestic sales this past year have been nonexistent. We haven't picked up a major new client in close to a year. And some of our current customers are jumping ship. We need to get them back, as well as drum up new business."

"What do you want me to do?"

"I've been soliciting a new client. His name's Raven Sierra, and he owns a string of ranching co-ops. I've almost convinced him to test a Gem-type security system. Assuming he agrees to a trial run and all goes well, he plans to purchase the system for both home and office. That will give us a whole new niche of the market to explore."

"Sierra has that much influence?" At Nick's nod, she asked. "How can I help?"

"I'd like you to show him how simple Gem is to operate."

Dani couldn't help it. She laughed. "You've got to be kidding."

"He wants to be certain that his daughter won't have a problem with the system."

"In that case, you'd be better off having this conversation with your computer."

"How many times do I have to tell you—"

"I know, I know. Gem's a machine. She performs functions she's been programmed to follow."

"Exactly."

"No thought. No emotion. Just circuit boards and memory chips. Right, Nick?"

His mouth tightened. "Just like Gem's creator."

That stopped her, reminded her of the true reason for her visit—to discuss last night's phone conversation. "That's not what I said."

"No?" He shoved back his chair and stood. "It's what you meant, though. Isn't it?"

She straightened, eyeing him warily. "For some reason you're determined to turn this marriage into a real one. But it's not. We had one night together. That's all it was."

He crossed to the window, his back to her. "One spectacular night."

"Fine. One spectacular night." Her comment was supposed to sound calm. It didn't. Memories pierced every word she spoke. "But it's not enough of a foundation for marriage. There has to be trust and...and emotional commitment."

He turned. "And Abigail? Is she enough of a foundation?"

"Perhaps," Dani conceded. "If things had been different."

"Specify."

She shook her head. "Do you hear yourself, Nick? 'Specify?' You can't just bark orders at me and expect me to input or output or compute some function. I'm a woman."

His mouth tilted. "Do you think I don't know that?"

"No. I don't think you do." How could she make him understand? "I'm not Gem. You can't push a button or program certain functions in order to turn me into a model wife. I'm not a machine, Nick. I want more."

"Tell me what you want." It was a demand, spoken with a cutting edge. She could see the frustration seething beneath the calm. But as always, he kept it under control. Tight control. "Name it and it's yours."

"I..." She closed her eyes, struggling to speak dispassionately. Then, realizing why, she released a wobbly laugh.

"I'm sitting here, trying to compose a logical argument. I'm trying so hard not to get emotional, because I know that's not something that makes sense to you or that you'd appreciate. There's only one problem." She lifted her gaze to his. "That's who I am. I'm an emotional person, Nick. You programmed Gem to alert you when I deviate. But what you don't seem to realize is that I deviate all the time.''

''Do you think I don't?''

''As far as I'm aware, it only happened once.''

His face settled into harsh lines. And his eyes— Her breath caught. Oh, heaven help her. His eyes blazed with more emotion than she'd ever thought possible. He approached her with unmistakable determination.

Her hands tensed on the armrests of her chair. ''Nick, don't.''

''Once? Do you think that was the only time? Well, guess what?'' Reaching down, he yanked her into his arms. ''In case you haven't realized, wife, I'm deviating right this minute. I'm deviating like you wouldn't believe.'' His mouth hovered over hers, and he thrust his hands deep into her hair. ''I want you, Dani. I want you in my arms. I want you in my bed. But most of all I want you in my life.''

And then he kissed her.

It was rough with desperation, raw with need. He consumed her, drank her in, savored the rich, sweet taste. And she was helpless in his arms. No. Not helpless. She could step away at any point. But she didn't want to. Heaven help her, she couldn't bear to leave the Eden he'd created. It had never been like this with Peter. Never. They'd experienced passion. But not on this level, not to this height or depth or degree. They'd been children, playing at love.

This consuming force couldn't compare. With every kiss, every nip of his teeth and slide of his tongue, Nick proved that what they felt went beyond mere passion. There was a terrifying commitment in his touch, a gentle entreaty beneath the savage demand.

''What do you want from me?'' Her question was almost lost within his kiss.

But he heard, heard and understood. His hands cupped her face, and he seared her eyelids with his lips. Then he sipped from her mouth one last time, a heart-rending tribute to emotions she was determined to deny. "I'll take whatever you have to give," he said. "I want it all. But I'll take whatever you have left."

Tears filled her eyes. "Don't you understand? I don't *have* anything left."

"You have more than you realize. You're just afraid to trust me." His hands slipped to the sides of her breasts and hesitated. Then his thumbs softly, ever so gently, traced the burgeoning tips. "Isn't this enough for you, Dani?"

"All it proves is that you want me. I already knew that." A tear escaped, the hot splash scalding her cheek. "Peter wanted me, too. Briefly. My mistake was thinking *want* meant *love*. I was seventeen and honestly believed I'd found my soul mate. I gave him everything within me to give. And he took. And he took and took and took until I had nothing left. That's when I realized—" Her voice broke, but she struggled on. "That's when I discovered that he didn't love me, had never loved me and never would."

"Dani, don't—"

"Do you know what his last words to me were? He said—" She dragged air into her lungs. "He said, 'Well, sweet cakes. It was fun for a while there. But you had to know it wouldn't last.' He smiled when he said it, like he expected me to laugh at some great joke. And when I didn't, he gave me this pitying look and said, 'Next time find someone who believes in love.'"

Nick wrapped her in his arms. "He's gone, Dani. He can't hurt you anymore."

"He was right." A fierce determination chased the pain from her voice. "Maybe for the first time in his life, he was right. Next time I commit to a man—assuming I ever trust enough to make that sort of commitment—it will be to someone who can love me as much as I love him. I won't settle for anything less. Never again.''

''MR. COLTER?'' Gem swept into the conversation like a cold wind heralding the return of winter.

''What is it?'' he rasped.

''PRIORITY ONE MESSAGE RECEIVED.''

''Relay.''

Instantly a woman's brisk voice filled the room. ''Take a message, computer,'' she said. ''Dinner. Six on Friday.''

''END MESSAGE.''

Dani moistened her lips. ''Who's that?''

The change in Nick was instantaneous. It only took one glance to realize that he'd returned to his arctic homeland. A bitter chill ate at the desperate heat from moments before. He crossed the room, distancing himself. ''That's my mother.''

She couldn't conceal her astonishment. ''Your mother.''

''I do have one. And a father, too.'' He offered a humorless smile. ''Oh, that's right. You thought I'd been assembled with bits of wire and electrical tape.''

She ignored his sarcasm. ''I thought they were dead. You've never mentioned them, and I got the impression—''

Nick's mouth twisted. ''They're not dead. At least, not physically.''

''I don't understand.''

''It's not important. I assume the invitation is for all of us. I'm sure they'd like to meet my wife and daughter.''

''I'd love to meet them, too. I'm just sorry they

couldn't make the wedding." A sudden thought occurred. "You did...you did invite them, didn't you?"

He laughed then. A sound so totally devoid of amusement that it frightened her. "What the hell do you think?"

And it was then she remembered him standing in the open doorway of the judge's office. He'd glanced up and down the corridor, hesitating for a brief moment before joining them for the ceremony. Waiting.

Waiting for his parents?

"LEVEL ONE SECURITY ALERT IN PROGRESS. FEMALE OFFSPRING UNIT EMITTING HIGH-PITCHED CRYING NOISE. PLEASE RESPOND IMMEDIATELY."

Dani fought for patience. "Yes, Gem. I know Abigail is crying. She's crying because I'm changing her diaper."

"SEVERE NOISE EMISSION HAS BEEN PROGRESSING FOR ONE POINT THREE MINUTES. RECOMMEND OFFERING IMMEDIATE NOURISHMENT."

"I just fed the baby. She's not hungry." Though why she bothered to argue with this font of mechanical idiocy escaped her. She'd learned long ago it was an exercise in futility.

"MY INSTRUCTIONS ARE SPECIFIC. YOU ARE TO BE NOTIFIED WITHIN THREE MINUTES FROM COMMENCEMENT OF CRYING NOISE."

"I'm to be notified *after* three minutes, not within, and you know it."

"NOISE INDICATES IMMEDIATE ATTENTION IS REQUIRED. PLEASE OFFER FEMALE OFFSPRING UNIT SUFFICIENT NOURISHMENT TO CANCEL ALERT."

Dani glared at the nearest speaker—not that it did any good. Glaring at a disembodied voice didn't provide the least amount of relief. What she wanted was a mechanized body so she could give it a good, swift kick in the microprocessor. "Abbey's receiving immediate attention, in case your warped circuitry hasn't processed that fact. Now cancel the alarm."

"ERROR NUMBER ONE-ZERO-SEVEN," Gem retorted, punctuating her comment with a snippy beep.

In response, Abigail increased the volume of her cries. "Now look what you've done." Dani took immense satisfaction in saying it. "She doesn't like it when you beep at her."

Instantly, a dizzying array of sounds poured from the speakers in the room. First Kenny G, then Mozart, ten seconds of Wagner, followed by a lightning-speed montage of Elton John. When none of that worked, Gem switched to people. "Cootchy-cootchy coo," blared Ruth's voice, followed by an odd compilation of Austin whistling various tunes. Next came Dani's sisters calling to Abbey in silly, high-pitched voices—the sort normally intelligent adults used only when coming eyeball-to-eyeball with a screaming newborn for the first time.

"Gem! Turn off that racket *immediately!*" Dani ordered. "It's time for Abbey's nap."

The speakers went dead. The next instant the phone rang. With a sigh, Dani plucked the portable from her pocket. Over the past four weeks, she'd learned to carry the blasted thing around with her at all times. Otherwise she'd constantly be running to answer the phone every time Gem ran tattling to Nick with another deviation.

"We've got a problem," he announced. "I'm on my way over."

"There isn't a problem, I promise. I'm not deviating at all. Gem—"

"This has nothing to do with Gem. We have a problem at SSI."

Dani held the phone against her ear with an uplifted shoulder. "What sort of problem?" she asked, snapping closed Abigail's red sleeper.

"I'll explain when I get there. Your mother's with me. She's agreed to baby-sit Abigail for the next few hours."

He'd picked up her mother? "It's that serious?"

"It's that serious."

"Okay. I'll be ready. I've just fed Abbey, so we can leave the minute you get here." She pushed the disconnect button, pocketed the phone and settled the baby in the crib. "Let her sleep, Gem. No talking, got it?"

Not that Gem listened. The stupid computer never listened.

The second she walked out of the room, she heard, "ONCE UPON A TIME..." uttered in Gem's version of a whisper. Dani groaned and headed for the kitchen to leave her mother instructions, along with Nick's cell-phone number. As an afterthought she scrawled, "If you have a problem, tell Gem it's a security one alert and the female offspring unit is deviating from normal behavior."

As soon as Nick's car pulled into the driveway, she greeted her mother with a quick hug and slid into the front seat. "So, what's up?" she asked.

"Remember the Toy Company?"

"Sure. Kit and Stephen St. Clair's business. They started down south in Carlsbad, then expanded and set up shop in Concord. We did their security system."

"That's the one."

"What happened?"

"It seems their system's gone haywire. They've called us in to correct the problem."

Dani's brows drew together. That didn't sound good. "What do you mean by haywire?"

"I mean the system has shut everything down. Kit and Stephen are trapped in one of the offices and can't break out."

"Uh-oh."

"It gets worse. They also have a day-care facility on the premises."

Dani's breath caught. "The children?"

"No one knows what's happening to them. Everyone's either locked in or locked out."

"Which model did they purchase? I can't remember."

"A Gemini unit." He slanted her a wry glance. "In case you're unfamiliar with that one, it's less sophisticated than Gem."

"It may be less sophisticated, but I'll bet it has every one of her bugs," she muttered.

Of course, he heard. "Gem does not have bugs!"

"Oh, no? Then why was I force-fed Kenny G for two solid weeks?"

"How many times do I have to tell you? Gem's a computer. If you make a simple request, the computer obeys. It couldn't be any easier."

"If Gem's just a computer, then why do you refer to her as 'she'?"

"So I've anthropomorphized her."

"Sounds painful."

"It means—"

Dani held up her hands. "I don't even want to know. Too kinky for my taste. And for your information, I do make simple requests. I make them all the time. But *she* never obeys. Would you care to guess why?"

His jaw tightened. "It's a computer glitch."

"You're such a man," she scoffed. "It isn't a computer glitch. It's plain, old-fashioned jealousy."

"What?"

"You heard me. She never listens to anyone but you—with the possible exception of the female offspring unit. She's taken quite a shine to Abigail."

"That's because I programmed her to monitor the baby."

"Oh, really? Did you also program her to talk to Abbey?"

"What do you mean?"

"I mean she goes in there and makes cooing noises."

"Her voice modulator must have developed another hiccup."

"A hiccup, huh? I guess that hiccup also explains the various Disney characters she imitates—not to mention the variety of music she's determined the female offspring unit needs in order to sleep. Or the fairy tales she's decided are essential bedtime stories. And in case you didn't realize... Remember that three-minute alarm you set?"

"If Abigail cries for longer than three minutes, Gem is supposed to notify you? That one?"

"Right. That one. Well, Gem feels—"

"Gem *can't* feel." He bit out the words.

Dani snapped her fingers. "Silly me. I'll rephrase. Gem has formed the undoubtedly logical and unemotional conclusion that three minutes is far too long for the female offspring unit to cry."

"When does she notify you?" he asked warily.

"I believe she sounds the alarm at the exact instant Abbey draws breath to let out her first squeak. Next I'm sure Gem will anticipate the moment Abigail *should* cry and alert me then."

Nick winced. "I'll look into it."

"Great. Now tell me that your precious Gem isn't to blame for shutting down the Toy Company. After all, computers don't run amok like they do in crazy science-fiction movies. And they certainly don't make their own decisions or form crushes on their inventors or go all maternal over female offspring units.''

"No, they don't," he insisted through gritted teeth.

"Hmm. Didn't think so."

They pulled into the parking lot, which brought an abrupt end to their discussion. Employees milled outside the entranceway, occasionally attempting to tug open the front door. As Nick and Dani started down the sidewalk, a tall, lean man broke free from the group and approached. She vaguely remembered him being introduced as the head of Testing and Research.

"Hey, Colter. Sure am glad you dropped by. We could use your help."

Nick held out his hand. "Hello, Todd. Good to see you, too. What's going on?"

"Oh, not much. Seems we have a computer gone berserk. Sort of reminds me of those crazy science-fiction movies. You know the ones I mean? Where the mad computer traps innocent humans in an office building and then proceeds to kill them off one by one?"

Nick lifted an eyebrow. "Gemini's killing off people, is she?"

"Not yet," Todd admitted cheerfully.

"But it's only a matter of time," Dani added.

Shooting her a quelling look, Nick stalked to the access panel outside the front door. Typing in a series of numbers, he announced, "System override. Colter zero-zero-one. Status report."

"GOOD MORNING, MR. COLTER," a Gem-like voice responded. *"ONE MOMENT FOR STATUS REPORT. SECURITY ONE ALERT. FULL LOCK DOWN IN PROGRESS."*

"Cancel security alert."

"AUTHORIZATION CODE?"

"Colter zero-zero-one."

"AUTHORIZATION REFUSED. ERROR NUMBER TWO-NINETEEN. HAVE A GOOD DAY, MR. COLTER."

Dani couldn't help it.

She laughed.

Nick glared at the panel, not quite believing what he'd heard. "What the *hell* do you mean authorization denied?"

"Told you."

He ignored his dear wife. It was difficult, but he managed. "This is Colter, authorization code zero-zero-one. Recalibrate."

"AUTHORIZATION DENIED."

"You can't deny my authorization, you mechanical hunk of—"

"DENIED! DENIED! DENIED!"

Beside him, Dani snickered. The urge to cut loose with a blistering expletive almost overwhelmed him. He struggled to regain his control. "To hell with that," he snarled. "Dani, get my cell phone out of the car."

"Like a good little wife?"

At that precise instant he felt the most curious sensation he'd experienced in his entire life. A peculiar tingle started at the base of his spine, shot directly upward to his medulla oblongata and pulsed there for a brief moment before radiating throughout his skull. Slowly he turned. Dani took one look at his face and stepped backward.

"I think I'm angry," he said. His voice had acquired an odd, scratchy quality.

"You think?" She stared, her black eyes so huge they threatened to swallow her whole. "You mean, you're not sure?"

"My brain appears to be off-line, so it's a little difficult to determine at the moment."

She took another step back. He noticed the toy company's employees were also giving him a wide berth, spread out in a distant semicircle.

"Why don't I go get your phone?" she asked him carefully.

"Yes." He turned to confront the access panel. It blinked smugly at him. The tingle radiating through his skull increased to a series of hot, pulsing flashes. "Yes. Go. Get. My. Phone."

The instant he had it in hand, he dialed Gem. "Phone through to the Toy Company, modem line only. Enable back-door access, Colter zero-zero-one."

"SECONDARY AUTHORIZATION?"

"Authorization code, control at all cost. Show no mercy, Gem. None."

"ONE MOMENT. ATTEMPTING INTEGRATION."

"*DENIED!*" shrieked Gemini. "*DE—*"

"ASSIMILATION SUCCESSFUL."

"Go, Gem!" Dani yelled the encouragement.

Nick smiled grimly. "Unlock the front door and access internal speaker system. Colter voice command only."

"YES, MR. COLTER."

The door lock snicked open, and he glanced over his shoulder at Todd. "I want you to stand here by the door. No one is to be admitted. Is that clear?"

"Yes, sir, boss. Clear as transparent aluminum." He winked at Dani. "That's a *Star Trek* joke."

Nick picked up a rock and tossed it from hand to hand. To his secret amusement, Dani's eyes widened again. "Ready?" he asked.

"I think that depends on your plans for that rock."

''I plan to do this.'' He bent and shoved it between the hinge and jamb of the door. ''Todd, no one is to touch the rock, either. We'll go make a body count and get back to you.'' He glanced at Dani. ''After you, Mrs. Colter.''

She brushed past him. ''Real smart, Nick,'' she muttered beneath her breath. ''That crack just sent two women nose-first into the bushes in a dead faint.''

''Really?'' He glanced over his shoulder. ''Could have been worse.''

''Yeah? How?''

''If they'd fallen the other way, they'd have ended up in the fish pond.''

He caught her muffled laugh as they passed through the vacant reception area to the main corridor beyond. It felt good to hear her laugh. Too good. He had to keep reminding himself that these moments wouldn't last. He couldn't become too entangled in her life—not when it was a life he didn't have a hope in hell of sharing.

The offices in this area were empty, just as Todd had claimed. ''Gem, are you on internal speaker?''

''AFFIRMATIVE, MR. COLTER.''

He hung up the phone and pocketed it. ''Status report.''

''GEMINI UNIT CURRENTLY IN STASIS. ELECTRICAL SHUTDOWN ON LEVELS TWO THROUGH FIVE. ELEVATOR INOPERABLE. LOCK DOWN IN EFFECT ON ALL FLOORS. MECHANICAL ACTIVITY ON FOUR. MINOR LIFE FORM ACTIVITY ON LEVELS THREE THROUGH FIVE.''

''Turn on the power, Gem. Then deactivate the lock down.''

''UNDERSTOOD.''

''Where's the day-care center?'' Dani asked. ''I think that should be our first priority.''

"Gem?"

"FIFTH FLOOR, NORTHWEST SECTION. ROOM FIVE THIRTY-EIGHT."

"Looks like we hike it to the fifth floor." Nick glanced at Dani in concern. In the past four weeks, she'd lost most of the weight she'd gained during pregnancy. But that didn't mean she was a hundred percent fit. "Are you up for the climb?"

She offered her sunniest smile, the one that never failed to tie his gut in a schoolboy knot. "I'm fine, thanks."

He inclined his head toward the end of the corridor. "Then let's go. Gem? Can you unlock the stairwell doors?"

"AFFIRMATIVE."

He took the lead, preferring he be the one to confront any unexpected problems. Despite the urgency, he kept the pace slow as they started the climb, just in case Dani had overestimated her strength. "This lock down brings back memories, doesn't it?" The question bounced eerily off the cement walls.

"What? Oh, right. The Kilburn contract." Her soft laugh swirled up the stairwell ahead of him. "I think that was the longest three hours I've ever experienced."

Funny. It had seemed like the shortest to him. "Getting locked in that closet wouldn't have been half so bad if we'd had something to drink."

"Or a bathroom." Amusement rippled through her voice. "Gem sure did a number on us that day."

"It did teach me one thing." He deliberately paused on the third floor landing. "I learned to keep my cell phone with me at all times."

She joined him outside the stairwell door. Her breathing sounded slightly strained, so he stood there, acting as though they had hours at their disposal instead of minutes. "Did you ever figure out what went wrong?" she asked.

Nothing had gone wrong. Everything had occurred exactly as programmed. He wasn't proud of the subterfuge, but Peter had been out of the picture by then, and Nick had given in to temptation. Not that he could tell her that. "I guess it was just a—"

She grinned. "Computer glitch?"

"Right. A computer glitch." He allowed himself the luxury of a smile. "Some good came out of that incident."

"Really?" A hint of startled vulnerability dawned in the inky depths of her eyes. "What?"

She didn't fool him. Despite her brave words, she remembered full well, he was certain. They'd talked while they'd waited, learning more about each other in those few hours than they had in the previous few years. Finally, tired of standing in such a confined space, they'd settled onto the floor. She'd leaned her head against the wall and within minutes had drifted off. He'd slipped an arm around her, pillowing her head against his shoulder until she'd finally awakened.

That was the memory that lingered, even after all these months. Because in those first few cloudy seconds, in that fleeting place where dreams met reality, a sharp, bittersweet awareness had blossomed between them. He suspected it was the first time she'd actually seen him as a man. But not the last.

Definitely not the last.

"I'll tell you what was so special." He slipped a curl behind her ear, fascinated by the resulting hitch in her breath. "We managed to spend three whole hours in the same room without a single argument."

"Hmm." Turning her attention to the next set of stairs, she tackled them with determination. "I wonder what would have happened if we *had* fought. Maybe someone would have rescued us sooner if we'd started yelling at each other.''

Nick caught up with her just as she reached the fourth-floor landing. Glancing toward the steps leading to the fifth, he stopped dead. ''Hold it!'' Dani glanced over her shoulder at him, her bewilderment plain. In a lightning-fast move, he caught her by the waist and swept her behind him. ''Watch your step, sweetheart.''

''What is it? What's wrong?'' She peeked around him and gasped. ''What is *that*?''

''I'd say...a tarantula. A very big tarantula.'' The three-foot monster blocked access to the next level. It bobbed in front of them, its giant, serrated jaws opening and snapping closed. Something suspiciously like drool dripped from the shiny black pinchers.

''It can't be real, Nick. It's just a toy.''

''No doubt. But until I can ascertain what the hell it does, or what that goo is it's leaking, we're not going anywhere near it. Gem?''

There was no response.

''I don't think she can read us,'' Dani said. ''There probably aren't any speakers in here.''

''Then it looks like this is our first stop.''

He opened the stairwell door leading to the fourth floor. Matters weren't much better here. He and Dani stood pressed against the wall, watching as a battalion of tarantulas and mechanical men patrolled the hallway.

''What's the holdup, Gem? Why are the lights still off?''

''ENCOUNTERING DIFFICULTIES, MR. COLTER. REQUEST YOU MANUALLY DISCONNECT COMPUTER LINK LOCATED IN TESTING AND RESEARCH OFFICE ON THE FOURTH FLOOR.''

"Is that where the problems are coming from?"

"AFFIRMATIVE."

Dani tugged on his arm and pointed to a wooden door at the far end of the hallway. "Over there, Nick."

"Okay, follow me."

Running flat out, he hurdled the mechanical tarantulas barring his path and rammed the door full force. The sound of splintering wood rent the air as the door flew open and crashed against the wall. Nick stumbled across the threshold, rubbing his sore shoulder. Dani collided with him from behind, and he caught her before she went sprawling to the floor.

"I don't believe it," he muttered.

CHAPTER SEVEN

A PINT-SIZED BLONDE, not much more than ten years old, sat behind a computer terminal, huge glasses perched on the tip of her upturned nose. She swiveled in their direction as they plowed into the room, her huge golden eyes blinking from behind the oversize lenses. "Uh-oh," she said.

"Now there's an understatement if I ever heard one," Nick answered.

Twin boys, several years younger than their sister, stood behind the blonde. They pointed at the girl, speaking in unison. "Viki did it. We just watched."

"I'm going to kill her."

"Easy, Nick," Dani cautioned. "She's just a child."

"I'm still going to kill her."

"No, you're not." She planted herself between the two and spared Viki a sympathetic glance. "Her parents will do it for you."

"They can't. I got here before they did. That gives me first dibs."

If Viki found the conversation alarming, she didn't show it. Dani stifled a grin. That suggested the poor kid had heard it all before. Been there, done that? "Come on, Nick. Consider this good father training for when Abbey's a little older."

"I can fix the problem." Viki gnawed at her lower lip. "At least, I could if I had more time."

"Please. Don't bother. I'll take care of it for you." Nick crossed to the computer, punched in a series of

113

commands, then disconnected it from the wall. "Go ahead, Gem. You're clear to proceed."

"PLEASE STAND BY. ASSIMILATING."

"Status?"

"OVERRIDE COMPLETE. SCAN IN PROGRESS. ELECTRICAL SYSTEM NOW ON-LINE." The lights flickered to life. "LOCKOUT DEACTIVATED. ELEVATORS NOW OPERATIONAL. LIFE FORMS VACATING FLOORS TWO THROUGH FIVE AT A HIGH RATE OF SPEED. MECHANICAL OPERATIONS STILL IN PROGRESS ON FOURTH FLOOR."

"What mechanical operations?"

Viki adjusted her glasses. "She means the spiders and robots."

"They's guardin' us," Twin One explained.

"From bad guys," Twin Two added.

"Dammit!" The irate male yelp came from the hallway. A tarantula sailed past the doorway. "Victoria! You are in serious trouble, young lady."

"Daddy!" The twins took refuge under the nearest table.

An instant later Stephen St. Clair appeared in the doorway, breathing fire. "You are grounded for life! Longer, if I can manage it."

"Now, Stephen." Kit slid into view, struggling to shake a spider free of her slacks. "It was an accident, I'm sure."

Twin arms flashed out from beneath the table. Twin index fingers pointed toward Viki. "She did it!" they yelped in unison. "We just watched."

"Tattletales," Viki muttered.

Stephen turned to Nick. "I'm sorry about this. I don't know what the hell she did—"

"I accessed Gemini through a flaw in her authorization code," Viki answered.

Nick stared in disbelief. "You— How?"

"I typed in Colter zero-zero-one cuz that's what I heard you say one time to access the computer. I had to mess around with the program for a couple hours, but after a while I got it to respond. Then I started telling Gemini to do stuff, and she did."

Dani covered her mouth. If she didn't miss her guess, Nick was beginning to feel anger again. A peculiar noise issued from deep in his throat—a noise that sounded remarkably similar to the one Viki's father was making.

"I don't understand," Stephen said angrily. "Why couldn't I override the system? I thought *my* code controlled Gemini's operation."

Viki shrugged. "Mr. Colter's override overrides yours."

"Mr. Colter's override *always* overrides everyone else's," Dani added. She couldn't help it.

There was a telling silence. Then Nick addressed Stephen. "I apologize. It's a safety precaution, I assure you. At least, it's supposed to be. I'll return tomorrow and make sure you have a voice-activated override program, this time keyed to you and Kit." He raised his voice. "Gem, full computer wipe. I want Gemini cleared from the system. Reinstall with limited back-door access. Voice codes only, set sixteen."

"AFFIRMATIVE. MEMORY WIPE IN PROGRESS."

Stephen shook his head, a hint of a smile creasing his face. "I guess you didn't take my daughter into consideration when you planned this system."

"No, I sure didn't. Which reminds me—"

"You want Viki locked away for the next twenty years?" He glared at his daughter. "My pleasure."

"No." Nick grinned. "I want first right of refusal when she graduates from college. At a guess that'll only be in another five or six years."

"Better working for you than against you?" Stephen asked wryly.

"Something like that."

"What do you say, Viki? Would you like a job with Mr. Colter?"

"That depends." She gnawed on her lower lip some more. "Do I get to work with Gem?"

Nick inclined his head. "If that's what you'd like. Or you can create your own Gem."

Her eyes glowed like sunlight. "Yes, please!"

"Then it's a deal." He offered his hand. "Have your father call me this summer after school lets out. We have an apprenticeship program that might interest you."

"Can I use the computers?"

"Only the ones without direct access to Gem. The idea of you two working in concert is downright terrifying."

The next hour passed quickly. Nick verified that Gemini had been removed from the system and replaced with a modified version. Then they took their leave. Dani linked arms as they walked to the car. "That was sweet of you, by the way."

He lifted an eyebrow. "Sweet? Me?"

"Yeah, sweet. Kind. Nice." She slid into the passenger seat. "Generous not to beat Viki into the ground."

He frowned. "Why would I do that?"

"Because she tinkered with your precious computer."

To her surprise, he chuckled. "She did a good job, didn't she? Even Gem's impressed."

"She ought to be. That's one clever young lady." Dani yawned. "Time to get home, I'm afraid. Abbey will be hungry soon."

Nick started the engine. "Thanks for coming with me. You were a big help."

"I don't think I helped all that much, but it was my pleasure to tag along."

At least it was a pleasure right up until the moment she walked through the front door of her house and found her entire family busily packing her belongings into moving boxes.

"Could someone please tell me what's going on here?" Dani requested. Politely. Not that she felt terribly polite.

Everyone ignored her except Ruth, who glanced from the box she was loading and smiled. "Oh, darling. I'm so sorry."

"You're sorry?"

"I'm sorry we didn't think of this earlier," her mother clarified. "Do you realize it's been a full month since your wedding? Well, of course you do. Silly me." More items disappeared into the box.

"Would you stop what you're doing and— It hasn't been a month. It's only been four weeks."

"Exactly. Far too long." Ruth rocked on her heels and shook her head in amazement. "You've been so sweet, Danielle. You haven't complained even once, despite the fact that this whole situation must have been agonizing for you. So your father suggested we help out."

"Help." This didn't sound good. Not good at all. "I've lost you, Mom. Which agony are you all helping me with?"

"Why, the agony of moving, of course. Now don't worry, we're just getting some of the preliminary items out of the way this afternoon. The moving company will handle the rest. I'm afraid the earliest time they have available isn't until next Saturday. Will that be convenient?''

"Mother! Just…just wait a minute, will you? You still haven't explained *why* you're doing this.''

"Because you haven't had a chance to take care of it yourself. Darling, I don't mean to interfere—''

"Yes, you do.''

Ruth made a face. "All right. I do. But it's been a month since Abbey was born. All right, all right. Four weeks. The point is, I can't believe you and Nick are happy maintaining two separate residences.''

"That's none of your—''

"It's time you put your family first,'' her mother interrupted firmly. "It's time you finished moving over to Nick's.''

Dani didn't dare admit she hadn't even started. No sense opening that proverbial can of worms. "Don't you think he and I should worry about it?''

"No need,'' came the blithe retort. "Not anymore. And since Nick doesn't object, neither should you.''

"Did he… Did he tell you that?'' A horrifying thought occurred. "Did he arrange this?''

"Arrange for us to help pack? Good gracious, no. We offered. He said he'd take care of it when he had the chance.'' She clicked her tongue. "The poor man. Considering how hard he works, I doubt he'll ever find time.''

"Mom—''

Ruth beamed, waving a hand in dismissal. "No, no. Don't thank us.''

Dani sighed. "Don't worry. I won't.''

"It's our pleasure, believe me. Just think of it as another wedding present. You sit back and relax and take care of my granddaughter. We'll handle the rest. By next week you and Nick and Abigail will be one, big happy family snug under the same roof. Oh! And guess what?''

Dani didn't want to ask. She really, truly didn't. ''What?''

''The sheets for Nick's bed arrived today. Isn't that wonderful timing?''

''Wonderful, Mom.'' Dani groaned. ''Just gosh-darn-it-to-blazes wonderful.''

''GEM.''

Instantly the television monitor flickered to life, displaying the nursery at Dani's house. Nick didn't even need to specify his request. Visiting with his daughter each morning had become as much a part of his routine as his shower. Gem had assimilated that fact.

He toweled off as he watched Abigail. She lay in her crib, awake and content, studying her world with wide blue eyes. The mobile spun lazily overhead, dappled sunlight reflecting off the various Disney characters. The computer was keeping her entertained. He heard Gem speaking in her newly acquired ''whisper'' mode.

He grinned as he began to dress. Telling the female offspring unit fairy tales seemed to be the current favorite. *The Three Little Pigs,* complete with sound effects, was in progress. Abigail cooed in appreciation.

A few minutes later Dani entered the room. ''What's going on in here?'' she demanded, planting her hands on her hips.

''RESEARCH INDICATES THAT HUMAN OFFSPRING UNITS ENJOY THE RECITATION OF FICTIONAL STORIES ABOUT FANTASY CREATURES.''

''You're telling Abigail fairy tales again?''

''AFFIRMATIVE.''

"But, Gem, I've explained this to you before. She's too little to understand."

"FEMALE OFFSPRING UNIT DOES NOT COMPUTE?"

"No, Gem. She does not compute. Maybe when she's a little older." The phone rang, and Dani groaned. "Let me know if Abbey cries."

"REQUEST UNNECESSARY. CRYING RECEIVES SECURITY ALERT STATUS ONE."

"Right. Silly me."

Dani left the room, and there was a moment's silence. Then the screen flickered, switching to a view of the kitchen. His wife stood there, phone in hand, talking to her mother, if he didn't miss his guess. He frowned. What the hell were all those boxes stacked everywhere?

"Gem, you know the rules," he instructed, thrusting his arms into a crisp white dress shirt. "The nursery is the only room you're permitted to video unless there's an emergency."

"AFFIRMATIVE." The next instant, Abigail filled the screen again. A wolf's howl whistled through the speakers—a very muted wolf's howl—and the story resumed.

Nick shook his head. "Waiting until Dani's out of the way is very sneaky, Gem. I don't remember programming you with a stealth mode."

"PROGRAMMING ACCESSED AT THE TOY COMPANY," came the smug retort.

"We've discussed picking up stray programs before, Gem. It can compromise your system. Download file onto computer thirty-four. I'll examine it later. Screen off."

"AFFIRMATIVE."

Beside him, the phone rang. He knew without answering that it would be Dani. "Speaker on. Colter, here."

"Nick?" Her greeting escaped in a nervous rush.

"What's wrong, Dani?"

"I need your help. There's…there's a problem."

"I'm always happy to help my wife. What's the problem?"

He waited patiently and after a few seconds of silence, she cleared her throat. "The truth is, my parents were here yesterday and they've packed up most of my belongings."

Nick kept the amusement well clear of his voice as he worked the buttons of his shirt. "Are you moving somewhere?"

"Dammit, Nick! You know I am. Mother said she spoke to you about this. About us moving in together, I mean."

"Yes, she did. As I recall, I told her I'd take care of it."

"Well, apparently you didn't take care of it fast enough," Dani retorted acerbicly. "My stuff arrives at your place on Saturday."

"Okay." He selected a tie from a rack in his closet. "You said there was a problem. What is it?" The speakers caught and reflected her sharp inhalation of breath. If he didn't miss his guess, his lovely bride was somewhat annoyed. He grinned.

"What is— I *can't* move in with you! That's what the problem is."

"Sure you can, sweetheart."

"That isn't part of our agreement."

"It wasn't part of *your* agreement." He knotted the tie, tacking it in place with a gold-plated piece of mother board. "It was always part of mine."

"Nick—"

"What do you expect me to do, Dani? Find a way out for you?" His humor faded. "I don't want to find a way out. I want my wife and daughter here, living with me in my home."

"I should have known you wouldn't help!"

"Yes. You should have. I'll see you Friday."

"Friday?"

"Don't tell me you've forgotten we're having dinner with my parents."

"I haven't forgotten."

He could hear the lie in her voice. It instantly restored his humor. "Good. Which reminds me. Sounds like moving day will be a busy one. Raven Sierra and his daughter will be joining us that night for dinner. You're supposed to show him how easy Gem is to operate, remember?"

"Dammit, Nick!"

He snagged his suit coat from a wooden hanger. "Yes?"

Her sigh of resignation slipped across the line. "What time Friday?"

"Five-thirty. And, sweetheart?"

"What?"

"Checkmate."

The phone banged down in response. But not before he heard her muffled laugh.

"We need to stop and pick up Chinese at the restaurant on the corner."

"Are you sure?" Dani asked. "I thought your parents invited us for dinner."

"They did."

"Then why are we picking up take-out?"

Nick shrugged. "Because it'll save time."

"Oh. Is...is your mother that bad a cook?"

"It's possible she's improved since I last ate there. But I doubt it. Don't worry, Dani. You won't starve."

"It's not that. I just don't want to offend her."

"We won't."

Clearly, he didn't intend to discuss it, so she decided to let it go and judge for herself. She'd looked forward to meeting his parents, hoping they'd offer some clue to Nick's background. Although she'd often discussed the business with him, and on occasion his recent history, his past remained a mystery. Perhaps she'd finally learn why he worked so hard to suppress his emotions. Perhaps his parents could explain it to her.

After picking up dinner, they wound a circuitous path through Berkeley. Eventually they pulled up outside a huge house surrounded by a wrought-iron gate perched high on the hillside.

"Good grief, Nick. Is this where you grew up?" she asked.

"Right here."

She peered at the weathered facade. Unlike the other homes in the area, this place desperately needed a face-lift. It huddled in the shadows, dark on the inside as well as out. A monstrous holly loomed on one side, a magnolia on the other. Overgrown bushes partially blocked the path to the front door. If there'd ever been a lawn, it had long ago been overrun by weeds.

Dani shivered. "How old is this place?"

"Over ninety years. It was built right after the 1906 earthquake."

"That's amazing."

"Politely put." He set the emergency brake and turned off the engine. "This house is like an old woman struggling to hide her years behind too much makeup. No matter what artifice she uses, she still looks every bit her age."

As much as Dani wanted to disagree with his assessment, Nick had made an apt comparison. Still, it troubled her. He'd grown up in this house. The "old woman" he'd described had been part of his life. How much had it influenced the man he'd become?

"It's after six," she said. "Shall we go in?"

"Why not? If you'll grab the diaper bag, I'll get Abigail."

Dani picked her way along the walk and climbed the sagging wooden steps to the porch. Beveled windows flanked the front door, and she peered through the glass, unable to detect light or life on the far side.

"Don't bother with the doorbell. It hasn't worked in years. Knock." He shifted Abigail to his other arm. "Loud."

She pounded on the heavy oak. Silence met her efforts. "What now?"

"Take the baby."

He transferred his sleeping bundle, then pulled keys from his pocket. Selecting an ornate gold one, he inserted it into the lock. Giving the oak a hard shove, he wedged open the warped door. Entering, he crossed to an old-fashioned wall switch and pushed one of the buttons. Dim light drifted across the imposing entryway.

"Did we get the date wrong?" Dani asked, uncomfortable in the confines of the tomblike house. "I could have sworn your mother said today."

He smiled grimly. "You heard the message. Friday at six."

"Then where—"

"They're here. Probably in the basement."

"This place has a basement? Isn't that unusual?"

He shrugged. "They jacked the house up and put one in before I was born. I guarantee, they're down there."

"In the basement."

"Right. In the basement."

"What are they, mad scientists?" she joked.

If anything, his gaze grew colder. "Yes. As a matter of fact, they are." He gestured toward the room behind her. "If you'll wait in the parlor, I'll get dinner out of the car and then go find them."

"You're...you're going to leave me?" She swallowed. "Here? Alone? With mad scientists running around in the basement?"

To her relief, a reluctant laugh broke free. "I won't be long. Try to make yourself comfortable."

Dani glanced over her shoulder at the shadow-infested room he'd indicated. "Just wait in the parlor?"

"Yes, my pretty little fly. Just wait in the parlor."

Reluctantly, she carried Abigail into the room and settled on the edge of a faded couch. It was reasonably clean, though she'd be willing to bet it hadn't seen much use. Everything had a formal, untouched appearance, faded, yet unused. What a strange, strange childhood Nick must have experienced. She wondered about his parents, trying to decide if he'd been teasing with his mad scientist crack.

Nick. Teasing. She sighed. Great. Mad scientists for in-laws.

A minute later she heard the distinctive sound of the front door being forced open. The painful squeal of the wood woke Abigail. Though the baby started, she didn't cry. Instead, she yawned and then found her mouth with her fist. She sucked contentedly, and Dani smiled, sliding her palm over the silky auburn hair.

How had she been so blessed? Peter had not only been unable to have children, he hadn't wanted any. He'd been quite adamant about it. Even if he hadn't become bored with their marriage, they would have hit a marital crisis sooner or later because family had meant everything to her and so little to him. And though she didn't blame Peter for circumstances beyond his control, she would have happily adopted a child or been a foster parent. But he'd denied her even that.

She studied Nick. How different he was from her former husband. If it hadn't been for a combination of serendipity and one unforeseen night of rapture, she might never have known the joys of motherhood—or experienced the unbelievable pleasure he'd given her.

"I brought in Abigail's car seat," he announced from the doorway. "You're not going to want to hold her the entire evening." He set it on the floor, then indicated the bag of food. "I'll put this in the kitchen."

"I'll come with you."

She didn't give him the chance to refuse, but stood and followed him down the hallway toward the back of the house. The kitchen was surprisingly large and had been modernized within the past twenty years or so. Nick opened the refrigerator door, and Dani's mouth dropped.

"What's all that?" she asked in a horrified whisper.

He peered into the refrigerator as though just noticing. "The usual. Experiments. Various chemicals that need to be kept at a low temperature. And mold. There's always lots of that around here. Some intentional." His mouth angled upward. "Some not."

"What, exactly, do your parents do?"

"I told you. They're scientists."

"I mean…" She eyed a glass beaker filled with a misshapen spongy object covered in an interesting combination of orange, blue and green mold. "What sort of scientists?"

"Mom's a chemist. Dad's a biologist."

"And they conduct their experiments here? At home?"

"They're not into explosives, if that's what's worrying you."

She couldn't stop staring at the beaker. "What about viruses? You know. Those new ones. The type that eat people from the inside out."

"They don't keep anything here above a biosafety level four. Honest."

Her grip tightened on Abigail. "Please tell me you're joking."

He glanced over his shoulder. The light from the refrigerator cut across his angled cheekbones and revealed the humor lighting his eyes. "I'm joking," he assured her gravely. "Don't worry. It's perfectly safe. They just don't believe in working for corporate America. It's a sixties thing, I think. They free-lance. Their lab is actually state-of-the-art."

"The one down in the basement."

"Right. The one down in the basement."

"Will we have to get them?"

He shook his head. "We won't be able to access the lab. It's sealed." He shut the refrigerator door and crossed to another wall plate, this one more high-tech than the model in the foyer. He punched in a quick code. "This'll let them know we're here. I installed it when I was a kid."

Sure enough, they soon heard footsteps approaching from the staircase off the kitchen. A minute later his parents joined them. Dani studied the two with interest. Mr. Colter had a similar build to Nick's, although he carried more weight and had a slight stoop. Their features and coloring, however, were nothing alike. Clearly Mrs. Colter had passed on those particular genes, sharing her blond-streaked hair and intense blue eyes.

"Introduce us to your guest," she prompted.

Nick folded his arms across his chest, instantly complying. "Dani, I'd like you to meet my parents, Ellie and Hugh Colter." He fixed them with a cool gaze. "You remember Dani, don't you?"

"Dani as in Danielle?" Hugh's brow puckered. "Hmm. That would be 'God is my judge.' I vaguely remember meeting a judge. Good to see you again, my dear."

Ellie shook her head. "Well, I don't remember. Refresh my memory. When did we meet her?"

"At my wedding," Nick explained.

"Hmm. No. I don't remember her being there." His mother frowned. "As a matter of fact, I don't remember your wedding, either." She turned to her husband. "When was it, Hugh?"

He shrugged. "Tend to forget those sort of details unless I write them down. Last year, wasn't it?"

"During the photosynthesis experiment? I don't think so. We couldn't possibly have gone then."

Hugh looked at his son for confirmation. "Could it have been in the spring? We had a spectacular failure with moss last spring. Were bound to show up at your wedding when the moss died."

"It was five weeks ago," Nick offered helpfully. "During the growth rate of rye experiments. Remember?"

"Ah, yes. The rye. Highly successful. Very promising. So what brings you here today, my boy?"

"Dinner."

"Wonderful!" He peered around expectantly. "What are we having?"

"You invited us, remember?" Nick switched his attention to Ellie. "What are we having, Mother?"

"Let me see." She opened the refrigerator. "Oh! It's Chinese tonight."

Hugh rubbed his hands together. "Good choice. Love

Chinese. Sweet and sour pork is my favorite. Is there any pork, Ellie?"

"As a matter of fact, there is."

Dani stood, silent and confused, listening to the bewildering exchange. Finally she couldn't take any more. "I don't understand any of this," she announced to the room at large.

Hugh offered a reproving frown. "Aren't academics strong in your family, my dear?"

"Apparently not strong enough. What I mean is, you seem to think we've met before." She glared at Nick. "We haven't. I'm Nick's wife. I think he neglected to mention that part. You don't remember our wedding because you weren't there."

"Well, of course not," Hugh retorted indignantly. "Not if it was during our experiments with rye."

"What I mean is… This is the first time we've met. Ever. You don't know me and I don't know any of you. Well, except for Nick and Abigail."

"Abigail?" Ellie glanced around. "Who's she?"

Dani held out her armful, thought better of it and cradled the baby protectively against her breast. "Your granddaughter."

"We have a granddaughter?" Hugh demanded. "I don't remember any granddaughter. When did that happen?"

"Last month," Nick supplied, opening cupboards and removing plates. "I called you about it."

"I haven't checked the machine for a while," Ellie said. "We probably haven't heard the news yet."

Nick paused to confront his mother. "If you didn't get my message, then why did you invite us to dinner?"

"Because it's a blue moon, of course," she stated blithely.

To Dani's relief, even Nick seemed bewildered by that

one. Thank heaven it wasn't just her. "A blue moon," he repeated.

"Right. The second occurrence of a full moon in one month, to be exact. Last time you visited you said we should get together then. I specifically noted it on my calendar. Tonight will be a blue moon, so I called."

An odd sound rumbled in his throat. "I said we *only* get together once in a blue moon. It was meant as a criticism, Mother." He took a deep breath, and to Dani's concern, all expression slid from his face.

"Abigail... Abigail... One more minute and I'll have it." Hugh's brows met over a prominent nose. "I'm almost there."

Distracted, Dani looked at him. "Do you know what everyone's name means?"

"But of course. Hugh, thought. Nick, victory. And Eloise." He smiled at his wife. "She's my very wise one."

"Dad has a photographic memory," Nick explained. "There isn't a list he hasn't memorized. It's just unimportant details that tend to escape him."

She caught her lip between her teeth. Was tonight's dinner one of those unimportant details? Judging by Nick's empty expression, it would seem so. "What can I do to help?"

If he caught the secondary meaning behind her question, he ignored it. "Why don't you put Abigail in her car seat and join us in the dining room. We'll get the table ready."

Hugh heaved a great sigh. "Ah, yes. 'My father rejoices.' Excellent choice. Is it a family name, Danielle?"

Her heart gave an odd lurch, and her gaze clashed with Nick's. "No," she said slowly, remembering her husband's words the first time he'd held his daughter. "*It's just a name,*" he'd said. "Nick chose it."

"Well, now you know why." Hugh nodded his approval. "I'm not the only one with a photographic memory, my dear. Stands to reason he'd choose a name that meant something."

"Nick?"

He didn't say anything in response. Not a word. No expression. No emotion. Nothing.

But it was a lie. Every bit of it. How could she not have realized before?

CHAPTER EIGHT

"NICK—"

"This isn't a good time, Dani. We'll discuss it later."
His eyes held a curious blankness, as though they were
focused inward, staring at some private landscape only
he could see. "Would you mind getting Abigail's car
seat?"

It seemed easier to agree than to argue, especially at
this juncture. But she fully intended to tackle him about
Abigail's name at a later date. It struck her as too important to ignore. By the time she'd done as he requested, the others had assembled in the dining room.
Nick poured wine into glasses, the elaborate cut crystal
sitting incongruously alongside the boxes of take-out.
Knowing she preferred to avoid alcohol while nursing,
he'd given her bottled water.

"I didn't think to buy any fruit juice. Sorry."

She didn't want him to apologize. Not for anything—not for the odd house, not for their odd reception,
nor for the oddest element of all, his parents. "Water is
fine."

"So, tell us what you do, Dani," Ellie requested.

"Right now I'm concentrating on motherhood. But
for the past five years I've worked for SSI."

"What's that?"

They didn't know about SSI? She frowned.
"That's...that's Nick's company—Security Systems
International."

"Oh, right. Computers. Do you program computers,
as well?"

132

"No. They pretty much defeat me. I'm in sales."

"I see. You sell computers."

"No, I—"

"How do you sell computers if they defeat you?" Hugh questioned abruptly.

Dani took a quick gulp of water. "You don't understand. I sell security systems."

"I thought you said you sell computers."

"No, I didn't."

She directed a harried look in Nick's direction, annoyed when he lifted his glass in a sardonic salute. "Good luck," he mouthed.

Determined to set his parents straight, she explained, "I sell security systems *run* by a computer."

"She sells alarms, dear." Ellie spooned rice from one of the cartons. "Like the one Nick installed in the lab so we'd know when he needed us."

Dani tried again. "They're a little more sophisticated than that. They'd have to be, to sell in such a competitive market. But we've done quite well. SSI is an international business, known around the world."

"International, huh?" Hugh mulled it over. "Don't your alarms sell domestically?"

Dani dropped her fork into the moo goo gai pan and glared. "Yes, they sell domestically. We have a lot of domestic clients."

"A damn shame you've had such limited success. Well, at least you tried."

"That's not what I—" She leaned across the table and spoke in a loud, clear voice. "SSI is *very* successful. *Nick* is very successful."

"You're his wife. Of course you'd say that."

"And they're not *alarm* systems. They're *security* systems. There's a big difference."

"I'd think it would be easier to sell alarms," Hugh replied. "Simple to install."

"And they run off batteries." Ellie cocked her head. "Does your system run off batteries?"

"Of course not!"

"Well, there you are, my dear." Hugh speared a cube of pork. "Alarms are easy to use. And affordable. A product has to be affordable, you know."

"Our systems sell like hotcakes!"

"Don't exaggerate, sweetheart." Nick spoke for the first time. "I suspect hotcakes sell much better."

Hugh nodded. "Very popular, hotcakes. Practically sell themselves."

"So does our security system! And I can sell them because Nick is so brilliant. I'm actually selling him."

"His IQ is remarkably high," Ellie conceded. "Just tipped the scales into genius, as I recall. Too bad he didn't go into biology."

"Or chemical engineering."

"He invented a computer program that thinks! Gem is an unbelievable accomplishment." Dani's chin wobbled. "Aren't you proud of him? Don't you care?"

"You're a passionate little thing. Not terribly logical, though." Her father-in-law smiled sympathetically. "We're not criticizing Nick, my dear. We're simply discussing his achievements—or lack thereof."

Dani shoved her plate to one side, her appetite gone. "For your information, your son is so clever and has sold so many systems, he's a damned billionaire."

"I don't think so," Hugh said kindly. "I suspect you've put your decimal in the wrong spot. Move it over three or four places and you'll be closer to the mark."

"He is too a billionaire. Aren't you, Nick?"

"I used to be a billionaire. I told you, business is off

right now. I'm now just a measly old millionaire. I barely rate a mention in *Men with the Most Bucks*."

"Why aren't you defending yourself?" Her voice had grown husky and ripe with bewildered pain.

He took a sip of wine, his gaze surprisingly gentle. "What's the point?" he said at last.

Tears started in her eyes and clung to the ends of her lashes. In another minute, she'd thoroughly disgrace herself. "Now look what you've done!" She threw her linen napkin onto the table. "You've made Abigail cry."

She swept the sleeping baby into her arms and retreated to the parlor. It was time to nurse, anyway, assuming she could calm down enough to accomplish the feat. Unbuttoning her blouse, she found herself longing for Kenny G's soothing saxophone for the first time in weeks. Somewhere deep in the house an alarm rang. She heard the scrape of chairs and the murmur of voices, followed by stark silence. She shut her eyes and struggled to relax. Not that it did any good. Abigail whimpered.

"You and me both, sweet pea," Dani murmured unhappily.

The next instant she felt the couch dip beside her, then warm hands cupped her shoulders. "Relax."

She sniffed. "I don't think I can."

"I'll help. Lean against me."

The minute she'd done so, he eased her and Abigail onto his lap. She dropped her head to his shoulder and sighed. "No music?"

"I haven't installed Gem over here. She wouldn't like living here, and my parents wouldn't enjoy having her."

"I'm with Gem." Then, realizing she'd been overly critical, she apologized. "I didn't mean that the way it sounded."

"I know what you meant."

"Nick—"

"Forget about it, Dani. I shouldn't have brought you. My parents... They take some getting used to."

"But—"

"Let it go. If you keep worrying, you won't be able to nurse."

She nodded, her cheek brushing against the fine cotton of his shirt. He felt warm and solid and utterly calm. Her tension eased slightly. "Everything seems to get clogged whenever I'm upset," she confided.

"I know." His hand slipped under her hair, and he rested his chin on the top of her head. "Let's see what we can do about that."

"Where are your parents?" She made a face. Apparently she couldn't drop the subject. At least not yet.

"They went back to the lab."

"Oh." She peeked up at him. "Was it my fault?"

"No. Didn't you hear the buzzer? Their latest experiment is at a crucial point. They had to get downstairs."

"Oh," she said again. And then, "Did that happen a lot when you were growing up?"

"I was a very independent child."

"Out of choice...or out of necessity?"

Nick pushed a tumble of dark curls from her forehead. "Does it matter?"

He said it so stoically, with such utter fatalism, it took everything she had to respond with a matching tranquility. "If it didn't matter, I wouldn't ask."

His sigh emanated from a spot deep inside, from a place she suspected had long ago been protectively encased in ice. "My parents have always been very involved in their experiments. As a result, they didn't have a lot of spare time. I learned early on that the fastest and easiest way to get something done was to do it myself. Does that answer your question?''

Her brow wrinkled, and she swung her foot back and forth. It must have been a very different existence from the one she'd experienced. With so many brothers and sisters demanding attention, her parents couldn't have escaped to a basement retreat even if they'd wanted to. They were constantly on the run, chauffeuring kids to dance recitals and sporting events and school— Her frown deepened.

"How many of your school activities did Hugh and Ellie make?"

"Don't, Dani. There's no point."

"How many, Nick?"

"They came to some." A rough laugh rumbled deep in his chest. "They just showed up a little late."

The hand not holding Abbey caught his shirt and curled into the soft cotton. "Like at our wedding?" she whispered. "That sort of late?"

"Yeah."

Just that one word. But it told her everything she needed to know. She could picture it. Every bit of it. A lean, towheaded boy with needy eyes and an oddly closed expression. He'd come home from school to an overgrown yard and a dark house. It probably took all his strength to shove open the front door. And inside he'd find...silence. No lights, no appetizing odors from the kitchen. Just a refrigerator full of chemicals, experiments and mold, and parents who spent their lives in the basement. If hunger struck, he'd fix himself a meal. If he needed help with his homework, he'd ask a neighbor. And if he longed for a hug or a pat on the back? What then?

She screwed her eyes shut against the pain, unable to stop the path of her thoughts. When Nick was still a child, he'd installed an alarm. If his need for attention grew desperate enough, he'd push a button. She doubted he'd often given in to the lure of that button. But once he had, he'd undoubtedly been forced to wait. He'd stand by the steps leading to a dark, sealed basement. And wait. He'd probably spent a lifetime waiting. Always waiting. Forever disappointed.

An image filled her mind. An image of Nick on their wedding day. He'd hesitated in the doorway between the corridor and the judge's chambers, delaying the ceremony. Hoping against hope that his parents would come?

This time she couldn't stop the tears.

He tensed, every muscle rigid. "I don't want your pity, Dani. I don't want it, nor do I need it."

"What do you need?"

"This."

His mouth closed on hers, parting her lips with gentle insistence. This was a far different give and take than the exchange in his office. The spark that day had been fast and almost painfully hot. Desire had raged, coiling and twisting tighter and tighter until it had been almost impossible to stop. But this kiss was unique.

It was tender instead of hard, a benediction instead of a demand. Nick's arms held her and their daughter with exquisite care, his mouth tasting of wine and ginger. With a soft sigh, she dropped her head to his shoulder and relaxed into his embrace, the stress generated from dinner slipping away. He pushed her shirt open and palmed her milk-laden breast, his thumb stroking the sensitive tip. It was the most erotic moment she'd ever experienced, and her response was as instantaneous as it was unmistakable. A familiar tingle shot through her veins, and his hand grew moist.

"You're milk's come in." Satisfaction lit his words,

and he cupped Abigail's head, lifting her toward the source of her nourishment. "There you go, sweet pea. Dinner's on."

Dani closed her eyes, more comfortable than she could have believed possible. She nestled deeper into Nick's embrace, a wistful thought disturbing the pleasure of the moment. How could she turn this fantasy into reality? She had a husband and a child—she should be satisfied. Instead, she yearned for more. She wanted a real marriage and a husband she could trust. But more than that...

She wanted love.

Nick's love.

Her breath stopped, and in that instant the terrifying truth struck. No. Oh, no, no, no. She wanted the marriage to become a reality because somehow, at some point, she'd fallen in love with her husband. Totally. Irrevocably. And forever. Her anger at his parents and her concern for his well-being stemmed from love. But her fear of living with him and her fight to hold him at a distance stemmed from fear—fear that once again, she'd opened her heart and soul to a man unable to return her feelings. Only this time she wouldn't escape relatively unscathed, as she had with Peter. If Nick couldn't love her, she'd pay a heavy price. She'd pay the ultimate price.

Nick made sure the front door to his parents' house was securely locked. Satisfied, he stood on the porch for a brief moment and surveyed the desolate front yard. It hadn't changed in years. Once, long ago, he'd made a stab at turning the brown, weed-choked garden into something green and living. But it had been a fruitless pursuit. The ground had refused to yield to him.

"Nick, are you coming?"

His gaze lifted from the barren yard. Through the cold iron gate he could see Dani. She waved at him and then leaned into the car, strapping Abigail's carrier into the back seat. A very attractive backside waggled back and forth and for an instant time seemed to slow.

Behind him rose his childhood home, darkly outlined against a dusky fall sky. And as he stood there a solitary leaf drifted before his eyes, trembling within the grip of a brisk wind. But he didn't move, refused to acknowledge the sudden chill or the rapidly gathering darkness. Refused to allow the emotions battering at his soul to escape.

"What do you need?" she'd asked.

He'd known the answer. He'd just been unable to explain, to admit what he needed to survive. The words had long ago been ripped from his vocabulary, just as the emotions they expressed had been ripped from his soul.

Dani approached the cold iron gate and gripped it with her warm hands.

"Nick! What are you waiting for?"

He drew a ragged breath. His jaw clenched and his hands collapsed into fists. There was life on the other side of that gate. An abundance of rich, nourishing life.

That's what he needed. If he was ever to find his way out of the cold, he needed what lay on the far side of the gate.

"I'm not waiting for anything," he announced, determination seizing him. "Not anymore."

Dani kicked the cartons stacked at her feet. "I'm telling you, Nick, I can't fit another box into the spare bedroom. I'm going to have to crawl over stacks of them as it is just to find my bed."

"You don't have to sleep there. You know that."

"We've been through this already. I'm not sleeping with you. Now, where are we going to put the rest of this stuff?"

"The hall closet?"

"Not a chance. Raven Sierra might see it there."

Exasperation edged his voice. "What difference does that make?"

"You told me his former wife soured him on the institution of marriage. I don't want to exacerbate it."

Nick lifted an eyebrow. "You've lost me. How do boxes in the hall closet exacerbate Raven's poor opinion of marriage?"

She shook her head at his ignorance. "The boxes are bound to make him wonder. We've been married for five whole weeks. Don't you think he'll find it strange that I'm just moving in today?"

"Public opinion never bothered you before."

"Well, it does now." Though why, she couldn't say. She kicked the box again. Yes, she could. Ever since meeting his parents, she'd hated the idea that she might cause him any pain or embarrassment. He'd already had more than his fair share.

"I'd think he'd find the five-week-old daughter produced from our five-week-old marriage of far greater interest. Compared to that, a few boxes don't amount to much of anything."

She set her chin. "How about putting them in your office?"

"Not a chance. How about the baby's bedroom?"

"No. Your bedroom?"

He sighed. "Yeah. I guess. Let's get a move on, though. Raven's due in an hour, and we still need to get cleaned up."

She hesitated at the reminder. "I forgot to ask about dinner. Is there anything I can do to help?"

"Not a thing. I'm having the meal catered, since I knew we wouldn't have time to do it ourselves."

"The dinner's that important?" she asked uneasily.

"Important enough. Word is out over the fiasco at the Toy Company."

"But that wasn't our fault!"

He hoisted a box. "Sure it was. A security system should be secure. Our competitors are making quite a point with consumers over the fact that a ten-year-old child managed to crack our system and wreak havoc."

Dani winced. "Point taken. I guess we'd better do one heck of a sell job tonight."

"We will." His mouth tilted. "We make a good team, don't we, sweetheart?"

Her smile blossomed in return. "Yeah. We do."

Dani had just zipped her dress when Gem announced the arrival of their visitors. "EXPLAIN FEMALE OFF-SPRING UNIT SIERRA," the computer demanded.

"Raven's daughter? What do you want me to explain?"

"SIERRA UNIT WALKS AND TALKS. CLARIFY ANOMALY."

"Oh. River's older than Abbey. Access human stages of development, Gem. That should give you the information you need. Before long Abbey will be able to walk and talk, too."

"PROCESSING."

"Fine. Process away. But while you're doing that, I'm going to join our guests."

She found everyone in the living room and studied Raven Sierra with interest. He looked the way his name sounded—black-haired and craggy-featured. He stood an inch or two taller than Nick and had a lean, hungry appearance. He brought to mind a lone cougar she'd once seen. Wounded and starving, it had prowled close to civilization, as though sensing help could be found just steps away. But the animal had proved too wary to accept a handout, even though it meant certain death.

She couldn't help but wonder which Raven would choose—trust and salvation, or solitude and the emotional death that would eventually result. What had happened to cause such a reaction? He suffered her curious look with ease, scrutinizing her in return with an intensity akin to the cougar's. Then he held out his hand, his grasp cool and firm. She noted the cynical appreciation in his gaze. So, he was as world-wise as he was world-weary.

"A pleasure to meet you, Mrs. Colter." She noted a remoteness in his gruff tones, a signal that clearly announced, "Man off-limits."

"Please, call me Dani." She smiled at Raven's daughter. Poor little thing. Imagine having a father as sexy as sin, but who clearly had no intention of providing his daughter with a mother. "And you must be River."

The name suited the little girl. She was small, her movements like quicksilver and her eyes an odd shade between gray and blue. Like her father, she wore her dark hair long, the wisp of bangs drawing attention to her unusual eyes. She regarded Dani gravely for a moment, then offered a shy, gap-toothed grin.

"Would you like to see Abbey?" Dani offered. "She's sleeping, but you can peek in on her, if you'd like."

River didn't require any further prompting. She slipped her hand into Dani's, and they set off for the nursery. They walked in on a story-in-progress. "What's that?" River asked, wide-eyed.

Dani stifled a groan. "*Sleeping Beauty,* if I'm not mistaken."

The little girl peeked around the room. "Who's talking?"

"That's Gem. She's our computer. She does all sorts of things for us. She can turn lights on and off, lock and unlock doors, fix coffee or tea or cocoa. She can even cook dinner with a little help."

"Does she...does she talk to you?"

"All the time." Fortunately River was too young to register the dry tone in Dani's voice. "Would you like to speak to her?"

"Yes." She clasped her hands together, looking uncertain. "What should I say?"

"Anything you like."

River took a deep breath. "Hello."

The story came to an abrupt halt. "IDENTIFY, PLEASE."

At the girl's bewildered expression, Dani prompted, "She wants you to introduce yourself. Tell Gem your name."

"Oh. My name's River Sierra and I came to visit the baby."

With that one sentence she succeeded in cementing an instant friendship. Gem took great delight in telling River all about the female offspring unit. Apparently the computer had accessed the various stages of human growth and development. She gave River a detailed lecture—a lecture Dani called a swift halt to just before Gem started in on the particulars of puberty.

"Implement educational program for discussions with River. Set program at age-level six."

"AUTHORIZATION CODE?"

"I don't need an authorization code, Gem. Nick told you to accept voice command, and you know it."

"VOICE COMMAND SET AT SHERATON RESIDENCE, NOT PRIMARY COLTER LOCATION."

"You have got to be kid—"

"Problem?"

Dani forced a smile to her lips and turned to greet Raven, praying he wouldn't sense her annoyance. Yeah. *That* was likely, considering she'd practically been shouting at Gem. "Not at all. I'm just setting the computer so she keeps her discussion and language age-appropriate."

"It doesn't sound like it was a successful program set."

To her relief, Nick walked into the nursery. "My fault, I'm afraid. Gem, Dani's voice command is approved regardless of location."

"AFFIRMATIVE. RESET IN PROGRESS."

"There you go, River," Dani said. "If Gem says anything you don't understand, just ask her and she'll explain what she means."

"Can she tell me a story?" River darted a nervous glance toward her father. "Like...like a mommy would?"

Tension ridged Raven's squared shoulders, and Dani hastened to answer, wishing she had the nerve to sweep the girl into a motherly embrace. "Sure. Would you like to sit in the rocking chair next to Abbey's crib? You can watch the baby while you listen to the story. If she cries, come and get me."

"REQUEST UNNECESSARY," the computer interrupted. "CRYING RECEIVES SECURITY ALERT STATUS ONE."

"Gem! Let River come and get us, will you please?"

The computer emitted a harsh beep.

Raven lifted an eyebrow, and Dani offered her most innocent smile. "That means yes."

"Of course it does," came the dry response.

Fortunately, Gem behaved herself after that. She

"played" with River and gave Raven a detailed description of her capabilities, as well as a demonstration. During dinner they discussed how the system would benefit the Sierras at home as well as in business. The frustrating part, as always, was determining the level of client interest. Dani found it impossible to tell. Raven had the uncanny ability to maintain as expressionless a facade as her husband.

Toward the end of the evening, Dani escaped to the kitchen to fix coffee, leaving Nick to answer some of the technical questions. The catering crew had long ago departed, leaving the kitchen immaculate. Everything gleamed a glossy high-tech black—the counters, the cabinets, even the appliances. Somewhere among all the black had to be a stove and refrigerator, but she was darned if she could tell where.

"Gem, do you know where the stove is?"

"AFFIRMATIVE."

Dani closed her eyes and counted to ten. Slowly. "Could you tell me where?"

"UNABLE TO COMPLY. THAT INFORMATION REQUIRES SECURITY LEVEL ONE CLEARANCE."

"You've got to be kidding!"

"ACCESSING 'KIDDING.' ONE MOMENT." An instant later, Gem announced, "KIDDING. TO JOKE. TO UTILIZE OR EMPLOY TEASING, HUMOR OR DECEIT IN ORDER TO TRICK. I AM NOT PROGRAMMED FOR THIS FUNCTION."

"Nick gave me voice command, you mechanical piece of garbage. Now tell me where the stove and refrigerator are right now!"

"UNABLE TO COMPLY. THAT INFORMATION REQUIRES SECURITY LEVEL ONE CLEARANCE. YOU ARE AUTHORIZED FOR LEVEL TWO ACCESS ONLY."

"What!"

Nick thrust open the kitchen door. "What the *hell* is going on in here? We can hear the two of you arguing all the way in the dining room."

"It's not my fault," Gem and Dani retorted in unison.

CHAPTER NINE

DANI GLARED at her husband. "Your computer won't tell me where the refrigerator is."

"Gem!"

"MRS. COLTER IS LIMITED TO SECURITY LEVEL TWO ACCESS. REQUEST FOR SECURITY ONE INFORMATION DENIED."

"Give Mrs. Colter level one clearance. From now on you answer her questions and obey her commands. All of them. Is that clear, Gem?"

"AFFIRMATIVE."

Dani folded her arms across her chest. "Now tell me where the damn refrigerator is!"

"PROCESSING. DAMN REFRIGERATOR IS TWO METERS TO YOUR RIGHT. DO YOU WISH ME TO OPEN THE DAMN DOOR?"

"Abso-damn-lutely," Dani snarled. "Then I want my husband to explain why kitchen appliances rate security one clearance. And *then* I want him to explain why I, his wife and partner, didn't already have it."

"This particular discussion will have to be postponed until after our guests have left."

The oddest sensation gripped her. Nick was hiding something. She couldn't say how or why she knew. She just did. She wanted to push him for an explanation now. Because by the time the opportunity arose again, he'd have a logical fabrication all ready to go.

"Give it a quick stab," she insisted. "I'm sure Raven won't mind waiting another thirty seconds."

He hesitated. "I'm the only one who's ever had se-

148

curity one access, aside from Peter's father. You've never had it. Nor did Peter."

"Why?"

"Because level one access enables you to change Gem's programming." His eye darkened, reflecting a hint of self-derision. "I think you can understand my reluctance to give up that much control."

He told the truth, she didn't doubt it. But not all of the truth. "All right, Nick. I'll let it go. For now." She turned to confront the blank expanse of cabinets. The refrigerator door stood open. Dani stared in disbelief. Gem must have done it. Wild. "Good grief. Have you shown Raven this?"

"I thought about it. But then I realized I hadn't shown you. Since you were so concerned about Raven finding out you'd just moved in…" He hooked a finger under her chin and eased her mouth shut. "Your reaction would have given the game away. Gem? Fix the coffee, will you?"

"AFFIRMATIVE."

At one end of the counter a black cylinder began to emit coffee-making hisses and burbles. Dani shook her head. "This is incredible."

"Glad you're impressed." He hesitated, then dipped his head and kissed her. He took his time, his mouth making a leisurely exploration of hers. Apparently he'd decided Raven could wait. "Welcome home," he said at last.

Dani clung to him, the possessive words singing with promise. For the first time in a very long time, hope returned to her life.

Night had fully furled, caging the house in what Nick had long ago termed a painful silence. He'd suffered periodic bouts of insomnia ever since childhood and often turned to work as a panacea. Work offered no solace tonight, however. An hour ago he'd listened to Dani creep into Abigail's nursery. More than anything, he'd wanted to join them. But he'd hesitated, uncertain of the reception he'd receive, even more uncertain of his ability to keep his hands off his wife.

Silently he left his bedroom and stood outside hers. The door was ajar, the bedside light burning. He entered, smiling when he found Dani sound asleep, a book open on her lap. Setting it aside, he straightened her covers. It would seem he wasn't the only one finding sleep elusive.

Luck had been with him the past few weeks. After five long years, he'd finally convinced Dani to marry him. She'd gifted him with a daughter. And now she slept beneath his roof, committed to a one-year marriage. Before long, he hoped to have her share his bed, as well. He had it all—everything he'd ever wanted.

Now all he had to do was find a way to keep it.

It wouldn't be easy. She didn't trust—thanks to Peter. Of course, she had more justification than she realized. In addition, she expected total commitment from marriage, and though he felt comfortable offering that commitment, she also wanted love. And *that* was something he couldn't easily give. He didn't even know if he felt such an emotion any longer. Physical desire—that he understood and could provide in abundance. But love? He shied from the possibility.

"MR. COLTER?" The computer spoke in whisper mode.

"What is it, Gem?"

"IS SOMETHING UNUSUAL HAPPENING?"

A small smile cut across his face. "No, Gem. I'm just checking on my family."

"THERE ARE NO DEVIATIONS IN PROGRESS?"

"Not so far." He reached out toward Dani, then hesitated. No. Not yet. Not until he could offer more than physical desire. His hand fell to his side. "Lights out, Gem. Alert me if she needs anything. Anything at all."

"AFFIRMATIVE, MR. COLTER."

The next two weeks slipped by with a swiftness Dani could scarcely believe. She hadn't known what to expect from marriage to Nick, how her newly discovered feelings would affect their relationship. To her relief, they hadn't caused any discomfort at all. In fact, an easy camaraderie had developed between them, helping to mute the underlying intensity.

Three weeks after their dinner with Raven Sierra, he agreed to give Gem a trial run. She and Nick worked together on the project, developing a closeness she'd never have thought possible. After they finished work each day, they'd sit together, talking and laughing about a variety of topics. Some evenings, they'd read or watch a video. But the most precious moments were those when they'd curl up on the couch together, Abigail tucked between them. Unfortunately, those occasions came far too infrequently.

She fought to keep her fears in check throughout the passing weeks, fought to convince herself that just because Peter had proved an unreliable husband, the same wouldn't happen with Nick. There was a depth to him, a strength and directness lacking in her former husband. Whether Nick was willing to acknowledge it or not, he had a deep well of emotional fortitude. All she had to do was find a way to tap into that well. A smile flitted across her face. To prime his pump. Until she found a way to back feed his lines and free what lay buried deep inside, she'd have to be patient.

Time. All she needed was time.

*   *   *

"Dani?" Nick exited his study. "Where have you been?"

She paused in the hallway, sensing his tension and surprised by it. "Oh. I guess I forgot to tell Gem. I had a doctor's appointment today."

"An appointment. With Abbey's doctor?" His tone warned of his displeasure.

Understanding was instantaneous. "I didn't steal a memory from you, Nick," she said gently. "I wouldn't do that. The appointment was mine. It's been two months since Abbey's birth and—" She broke off, a blush rising in her cheeks.

He visibly relaxed. "And the doctor gave you the all clear."

"Yes." She waited for him to say something more. To her relief, he didn't, simply nodded.

"I'm glad to hear you're all right."

"Thanks." Dani hesitated, shifting awkwardly. "I'll be in the nursery, if you need me. It's time to feed Abbey."

"Sure."

Nick stepped into his office but not before she saw a brief flash of longing darken his eyes. Acting on instinct, she asked, "Would you like to join me?"

He shook his head. "Somehow I don't think you'll be able to relax with me watching."

"I have every other time." It was true. He might make her a little self-conscious, stir feelings she fought to suppress. But he had the uncanny ability to help her relax enough to feed Abigail. "Are you sure? I don't mind."

He stood to one side. "If you're positive it won't bother you, then come on in."

"Here?"

"Why not? You can sit on the couch and tell me about your day while you nurse."

Having made the offer, she couldn't very well change her mind now. She refused to hurt him like that. How ironic. Two short months ago, she wouldn't have worried about his feelings. Heck, she'd never have even thought about them. How could you hurt someone without feelings?

Nick. Without feelings.

She perched on the edge of the couch and slanted him a curious glance. She'd known him for five long years, had believed implicitly and without question that he was no different than his computer. The idea seemed ludicrous now.

"Move over," Nick prompted.

He took over the far end of the couch and twisted into a reclining position against the armrest. He dropped one long leg to the floor and he extended the other the length of the couch. Then he patted the V between his thighs. She didn't hesitate, but allowed herself to be spooned into the narrow opening. The fit, as always, was delicious. He took Abigail from her as she opened her blouse and unsnapped the front clasp of her bra.

"Nick?"

"What?"

"You're not like Gem, are you?"

"Sure I am." He settled the baby in her arms. "We're two of a kind, sweetheart. Isn't that what you've always said?"

"Probably." Abigail latched onto Dani's nipple, suckling contentedly. "But you're not. I realize that now."

"What are you trying to say, honey?"

She didn't know. She truly didn't. A change of subject seemed in order. "What's that glass behind your desk?"

"A video monitor. The one in here is capable of displaying sixteen different images. The other rooms can only access one at a time.''

"There's one in every room?''

"Yes.''

"What do you monitor?''

"Anything that's connected to the video system. The house, the office. Television. Even some of our clients whose contracts call for it.''

"I didn't realize.'' She stiffened. "Wait a minute. Are all the rooms on the video system? Do they all have camera access?''

"Yes. If there's an emergency Gem will turn on the camera so I can evaluate the situation.''

"But she isn't taping all the time?''

"No. She only tapes when authorized.'' He paused, then released his breath in a gusty sigh. "I guess you should know that there are cameras in Peter's house, too. He asked to have them installed when I put in Gem. But he never activated them.''

After Abbey was born, Nick had connected his house with hers, Dani recalled. It only took a moment for the next logical question to occur. "Did you? Did you activate them?'' His arms tightened, as though to prevent her from escaping his hold. She knew what his answer would be even before he spoke.

"Yes.''

He said the word so softly, with such regret, that her surge of anger died before it was fully born. She eased Abbey from her breast. "Why, Nick? Why would you invade my privacy like that?''

"The first time was when you had trouble nursing Abigail.'' A rough quality had entered his voice. For a man without emotions, something about that incident had had a powerful effect on him. "Gem told me there was an emergency so I had her turn on the camera. You were sitting in the rocking chair crying almost as loudly as the baby.''

And as a result, he'd come running, racing from his house so fast he'd arrived with only a pair of hastily donned jeans, his keys and a burning determination to help. Still, she had to know. ''Were there any other times you had Gem turn on the camera?''

''Yeah.'' He shifted, the muscles of his chest rippling against her back. ''I'd look in on Abigail each morning. I'd watch her. Talk to her. Visit for a while. It was wrong. I knew it. But dammit, Dani. She's my daughter. I wanted to see her. Not just a few times a week, but every day. Can you understand that?''

''Yes, I can understand. But you should have asked, Nick.'' Dani decided to take a risk, to try priming his pump. ''You love Abbey, don't you?''

''She's my daughter.'' It was an oblique answer, at best.

''But you love her, right?''

He tensed. ''I'd give my life for her,'' he replied evenly. ''I'd do everything in my power to protect her from harm. I want to be part of her life and have her part of mine.''

''Say the words, Nick. Just say them.''

Silence greeted her demand, and she closed her eyes.

It hurt. It hurt more than she could have imagined. She'd been so certain, so positive he felt what she did. Everyone experienced emotions. Nick couldn't be so different, despite his childhood. He just hadn't found a way of expressing those feelings, didn't understand the significance of them. If only she could find a way to reach him, a way to break through the ice holding him prisoner. A way to prime that damned pump. She couldn't believe the man she loved incapable of loving her in return.

Why not? an insidious voice demanded. *Peter hadn't.*
The truth hit like a crippling blow.

Tears welled in her eyes, and Dani bowed her head.
"It isn't enough," she whispered. "I can't live like this.
I thought I could, but I can't."

She bolted from the couch, Abigail held tight within
her arms. Nick came after her. She sensed his pursuit,
heard his swift footfalls striking against the hardwood
floor. He caught up with her in the nursery, catching her
by the shoulders. He slipped Abigail from her grasp and
he settled the baby in the crib. Then he turned his attention to Dani, his gaze cold and remote.

"What do you want from me? What more can I offer
that I haven't already given?"

"Why did you make love to me? On New Year's Eve,
when I came here to give you those financial documents.
Why did you kiss me?"

"You know why."

"Desire?"

"In part."

"Was that all?" She searched his face, desperate to
find some clue to his innermost thoughts, some sign that
he felt something. *Anything.* "Did that night mean so
little to you? Was it just a fun romp to welcome in the
New Year?"

"I never said that."

"You've never said anything!"

She remembered that night, remembered how gentle
he'd been, how passionate and alive. There'd been a
hunger in his touch, a look in his eyes that told her he'd
been waiting for her—waiting a lifetime to make her his.
She'd tried to convince herself it hadn't been real, that
it had been part of a foolish fantasy. But still the hope
that it might be more wouldn't die.

Dani shook her head. "I couldn't have imagined the

connection between us. It couldn't have just been wishful thinking. I don't believe it. I *won't* believe it!''

''Words? Is that what you can't live without? You want sweet lies? The kind Peter told you?''

''No!''

''Or is this what you really want?''

He took her mouth, took it with hunger and demand and a poignant plea. He lifted her close, held her so she couldn't possibly mistake his reaction to her touch. He wanted her with a desperation that matched her own— powerful, total and utterly overwhelming.

''No, Nick. We can't.''

''We already have. Our daughter is proof positive of that.''

''That doesn't mean it's right. You don't love me. You don't even love your daughter.''

A muscle jerked in his cheek. ''I'm here. I'm committed to making this marriage work. I'm doing my best for you and Abigail. And we want each other. Can you deny it?''

Tears filled her eyes. ''No, I can't deny it,'' she admitted in a raw voice. ''But that doesn't make it right. It didn't when Abbey was conceived and it doesn't now.''

''We have ten more months before our agreement ends. Do you really intend to go through all that time celibate?''

''I'd planned to,'' she admitted with a watery laugh.

''Dani, please. Let's make this marriage a real one.''

''A real marriage is supposed to last forever. But Peter didn't want forever.'' She fixed him with a steady look. ''Do you, Nick?''

He closed his eyes against the wistful question. ''Peter was a fool. He wasn't worthy of either your love or your trust.''

"You haven't answered. Do you want forever?"

The question hung between them. He tensed, and she saw the rejection, the burning desire to brush her words aside. His expression tightened, closed over as it had so many times before. "I won't walk out on you and Abigail. I'll do whatever I can to make you happy. You can trust me, Dani. I won't let you down."

"And love?"

He didn't reply, and she knew it was up to her to decide. Could she live without love? She had with Peter. And who could predict the future? Perhaps love would come later, building over time. Perhaps she'd eventually break through, ease the icy hold on his heart, thaw it with her warmth. She could trust Nick not to hurt her. After all, he wasn't Peter.

He must have sensed her decision. Sweeping her into his arms, he carried her to the bedroom. Once through the door, he set her down. Dani stood in front of him, reading in his eyes what must also be reflected in her own. They were two wary people, both wanting to reach out, both hesitant to do so. Afraid to risk that final step forward.

She took a deep breath, suddenly aware that her blouse gaped open. She'd been so upset by their discussion, she'd forgotten to button it after nursing Abbey. Nor had she bothered to fasten her bra. Nick noticed, as well. Slowly he reached out, easing the cotton edges aside. She didn't protest, but allowed him to look his fill.

"You've changed."

She released a soft laugh. "Having a baby will do that."

"I want to see the other changes. All of them." He pushed her blouse from her shoulders and down her arms. The bra followed. His fingers danced across her erect nipples, circling the dusky bud. "They're larger. Darker." He palmed the weight. "And fuller."

A shiver chased through her. "Do you mind?"

"Not even a little. When we make love, will your milk come in?"

Surprised, she shook her head. "I—I don't know."

"I guess we'll find out together." His hands slipped lower. "I'm going to finish undressing you now."

She didn't answer, simply nodded in nervous agreement. He found the button to her jeans, parted it and lowered the zip. Tugging them down her hips, he crouched in front of her so he could lift first one foot free, then the other. She dug her hands into his hair, keenly aware that her only covering was a triangle of thin white cotton held in place by a sliver of elastic. She trembled.

To her surprise, he didn't strip her right away. Instead, he settled his palm on the slight swell of her belly, his hand warming her abdomen. "It's hard to believe that a few months ago, Abigail lived here."

"Hard for you to believe. Not so hard for me."

"I wish I'd been here for all of it. I would have liked to see the various stages of your pregnancy." He glanced up, his eyes a brilliant flash of blue. "Maybe next time."

"I'm not back in shape yet, and you're already talking about a next time?"

"I grew up all alone. I don't want that to happen to Abigail. I want her to enjoy a family like yours rather than suffer one like mine." He cupped her hips and brushed his mouth across the faint silver lines tracking her stomach.

"Skin runs," she explained with a wry laugh. "They're like runs in your panty hose, only worse. Unfortunately, I can't throw my skin away and buy a new one like I do stockings."

"In that case, consider them war wounds. Badges of honor. Besides, no one will see them but me." It wasn't a question, but a declaration of fact. "And I think they're beautiful."

Before she could comment, he finished undressing her, hooking his thumbs in the narrow elastic band of her briefs and tugging them down her legs. She should have felt vulnerable and exposed. But she didn't. Thanks to Nick, she felt beautiful and desired. He rose and stripped, each movement spare and economical. His shirt took the same path as hers, followed by his jeans. When he was through, they stood without covering or artifice.

And then they came together, their movements fluid and certain, rediscovering the secret places as they turned memories into reality. Her fingers slipped through the thatch of brown hair covering his chest while he hungrily supped on her breasts. When she molded the corded dip and curve of muscle and sinew, he heated the soft swell of her belly and thighs with his breath. And as she followed the line of his lean hips to trace the shadowed delta caged between his thighs, he cupped her bottom, drawing her home.

Wedding sheets covered his bed, and he lowered her to them.

They'd fought this moment, fought it even as they rushed toward it, driven by a tidal wash of desire. She opened herself to him, swirling her hips with earthy grace, capturing him between silken thighs. He planned to take it slow, she could see it in his eyes. But he could no more slow this storm than he could the one that battered them last New Year's Eve. He drove forward, planting himself deep inside, sliding along a path of unbearable sweetness.

His breath caught, blew hot against her throat. He

palmed her hips, his fingers digging into the curve of her backside. "I don't want to hurt you."

She shook her head, a tangle of dark curls spilling across the ivory sheets. "You'll only hurt me if you stop."

"Nothing can be this good."

"More could be this good. More would be even better."

He sheathed himself deep within her, rushing toward a desperate culmination, unable to stop or slow or turn back. She wrapped herself around him, struggling to absorb him, drinking his essence into her very pores. It didn't last, couldn't last, no matter how she might wish otherwise. She could feel the pull of completion, feel the slow tilt toward oblivion. And in that instant she saw past the shield that protected him from the world, saw his desire to give her all he had. The final explosion hit them. Hard. It was a benediction of touch, a joyous celebration, a melding of heart and soul. It had been nearly a year. Interminable months of emotional dearth.

But finally, at long last, those lonely months had come to an end. Her future lay within his arms, if only he'd allow it. First he had to find a way to release the love he kept safely hidden away, just as she had to find a way to tempt it forth.

When Dani awoke, it was dark. Nick held her close, practically surrounding her with his warmth. "Lights," she whispered. "Ten watts."

A soft glow lit the room, and she eased onto her back, turning her head so she could study Nick as he slept. Even in repose, he didn't relax, his expression still guarded. Masked. The times she'd managed to peek behind that mask had been few. She could count them on one hand. There were the two times they'd made love and two or three rare moments when she'd come upon him with Abigail. On those occasions, a desperate yearning had ripped apart his expression, proving what she'd long suspected. No matter how vehemently he denied it, he was a man of deep emotions.

Prime the pump. The words resonated through her. All she had to do was find a way to prime the pump.

Gently, she eased from his embrace, gripped by an inexplicable restlessness. She slipped on a nightshirt and padded into Abbey's room, but it wasn't time to nurse. So she hung over the crib railing, watching her daughter sleep, touching the rosy cheek. Then she trailed through the house, eventually wandering into the living room. She stood before the huge picture window, sensing the approach of dawn, feeling the gradual awakening clear to her soul.

It was like her love for Nick. It had always been there, hidden from view, waiting through a five-year night before breaking the horizon with heartwarming radiance. She stood perfectly still, caught in that breathless moment between night's demise and day's rebirth, watching as a pale, golden beacon seeped across the sky, storming the blackness.

"MRS. COLTER?"

"Yes, Gem?"

"IS ANYTHING UNUSUAL OCCURRING?"

Oh, yes, she wanted to cry. *Two years of dark are at an end, and morning has finally arrived.* A quick laugh reflected her joy. "No, Gem. Nothing unusual is occurring."

"DO YOU HAVE ANY REQUIREMENTS?"

The question caught her by surprise. "Why do you ask?"

"MR. COLTER REQUESTED I ALERT HIM IF YOU NEEDED ANYTHING."

"Not a thing." No, that wasn't entirely true. There was a question she had, one that Nick had never answered to her satisfaction. Something made her hesitate, though. Later, she'd put it down to a grim precognition. But despite that momentary qualm, the question tumbled free. "Gem, why is SSI in financial trouble?"

"ACCESSING. LOSS OF ASSETS RESULTED IN REDUCTION OF NET WORTH. FINANCIAL STATEMENTS AVAILABLE THROUGH MAIN COMPUTER TERMINAL."

She frowned. "Loss of assets? How did that happen?"

"ASSETS WERE ILLEGALLY REMOVED FROM SSI."

It took a moment for the full significance to sink in. When it did, a desperate foreboding gripped her. "Give detailed explanation, Gem."

"EXPLANATION REQUIRES LEVEL ONE SECURITY ACCESS."

"I have level one security access!" Her voice broke, reflecting her tension. "Now explain what you meant."

"PROCESSING." It seemed to take forever. Finally, Gem came back on-line. "FUNDS FROM THE FOLLOWING ACCOUNTS WERE ILLEGALLY REMOVED BY MR. PETER SHERATON. ACCOUNT NUMBER—"

"End transmission," Nick ordered.

CHAPTER TEN

DANI SWUNG AROUND, confronting Nick. "Is it true?" she asked numbly. "Did Peter embezzle money from SSI?"

"It's true."

"How? When?"

"The day of his death."

"You haven't recovered the funds, have you?" Her mouth trembled, and she pressed her lips together, struggling for composure. "That's why we're in financial trouble."

He hesitated for a telling moment before admitting, "No, I haven't recovered them. And, yes. That's why we're in financial trouble."

"What did he do with the money? Why couldn't you find it?" He turned away, and she frowned. There was more—and whatever it was, he didn't want her to know. "Nick?"

He ran a hand along the back of his neck. Finally he faced her. "The truth?"

"It would make a pleasant change."

"I did find the money. I chose not to recover it."

She could scarcely believe it. "Why? For heaven's sake, Nick! He must have taken millions."

"He did."

"Why didn't you get it back?"

"Sit down, Dani."

"No! I want an answer to my question."

"Sit down." He waited until she'd reluctantly complied before continuing. "He gave the money to Kristy Vallens."

"His assistant? But—" Comprehension dawned. "He was leaving me for her. That's where he was going when his car crashed."

"Yes."

"That still doesn't explain—"

"She was pregnant."

A wave of dizziness hit her. "No."

"She bore him a son. The two are currently living in Europe."

"No. She couldn't have. He was sterile!"

Nick's mouth curved in a humorless smile. "Apparently not. Tests were run, Dani. And though the odds were astronomical, it's true. The baby is Peter's."

"She must be lying. She must have used some of the money to falsify the test results."

He shook his head. "Why do you think I was gone so long? I had to verify her claim."

"How did you find her?"

"The papers you brought over on New Year's Eve gave me all the information I needed to track her down."

"Why didn't you have her arrested?"

"To what end?" His lips compressed, and deep lines bracketed his mouth. "Should I have thrown her in jail, turned her baby over to social services? Stripped Peter's child of his inheritance? Is that what you'd have done?"

It didn't take any thought. Slowly she shook her head. "The money was Peter's. Half of SSI was his, as well. I was—" She fought to speak dispassionately. "I was just along for the ride."

"If he'd come to me and asked to be bought out, I'd have done it. I suspect he chose to embezzle because Kristy's pregnancy caught them by surprise. They had to act fast or get trapped in endless litigation."

Dani bowed her head. "Even if he'd sold his share of the company to you, he'd still have left me."

"Yes, he'd still have left. And he'd have taken the proceeds with him before filing for divorce. You'd have had one hell of a time getting your hands on any of the money. He'd have seen to that."

"And I'd have been—" Broke. Financially destitute. Without a job or means of support. Her eyes widened, and she covered her mouth. "Oh, no."

Nick must have read her mind. He crouched beside her, catching her shoulders in his hands. "You're my wife now, Dani." He spoke urgently, stressing each word. "Nothing else matters. Peter doesn't matter. The money doesn't matter. We have our own life to live. We have Abigail. We can work through this."

"You've been supporting me all this time, haven't you?"

"I already told you. It doesn't matter!"

"Yes, it does." She set her jaw, fighting tears. "It matters to me. Why didn't you tell me?"

"For the same reason you didn't tell me you were pregnant. I knew you'd do something foolish if you found out." His mouth tilted. "Something noble and self-sacrificing."

"Damn you, Nick!" She gained her feet and stalked to the windows. Wrapping her arms around her waist, she turned to confront him. "You've made decisions about my life. Decisions you had no right to make."

"You did the same. Or have you forgotten the reason for our marriage?" He allowed that to sink in before asking, "What would you have done if you'd known the truth?"

"I...I'd have sold the house. That would have provided me with plenty of money while I looked for work."

"At the time of Peter's death, it was mortgaged to the hilt."

Panic gripped her. "No. No, it wasn't. We owned it free and clear."

Nick shook his head. "He mortgaged the house and took the assets along with the money from the firm. He actually had the nerve to have the monthly amount debited from an SSI account. It came through exactly three weeks after his death. That's how I found out. I bought the loan from the bank after the first deduction. Don't you get it? Peter didn't give a damn about you, Dani. He intended to leave you penniless. He did everything in his power to hurt you."

The tears broke free. "Why? Why would he have done that to me? I was his wife. I loved him. And he…"

Nick scooped her into his arms, enfolding her in a fierce embrace. "He did you a favor. Don't you see? If he hadn't left, you wouldn't have Abigail."

"And if New Year's Eve hadn't happened? If I'd never become pregnant? Would you have kept pretending that I'm your partner?"

"You *are* my partner."

She shook her head. "No. No, I'm not. Peter put an end to all that when he took the money." Pride gave her the strength to meet his gaze. "Answer the question, Nick. How long were you planning to keep up the subterfuge?"

"For as long as it took."

"Our agreement was for a one-year marriage. In ten more months you were supposed to buy me out. Only there's nothing to buy out. Was that your plan? To announce at the end of the year that there wasn't any money? That Peter had taken it?" She felt cold. So terribly cold. "Without funds, I couldn't leave, couldn't start my own business. I certainly couldn't support

Abbey. You'd have total control. You'd have us right where you wanted.''

He'd drawn inward with every word, returning to the Ice man she'd known a lifetime ago. ''Is that what you think?''

''I don't know what to think anymore! Our lives have been one big lie. How am I supposed to tell where the lies end and the truth begins?'' She pulled free of his arms. ''Why couldn't you have told me the truth? The only thing I've ever asked for was your honesty.''

''You don't want honesty. Because of Peter, you want a guarantee. You want the words, regardless of whether there's any validity to them. And you want me to give what I don't have. Where's the honesty in that?''

''You said I could trust you. Did last night mean nothing?''

His jaw tightened. ''If you want the truth, don't ask me to lie.''

It was all the answer she needed. ''Fine. No more lies.'' Dani curled her hands into fists. She wouldn't break down. She refused to allow the emotions he despised free rein. ''Is there anything else you haven't told me? Any more information I should have?''

''Just one last piece.''

She wasn't sure she could handle any more. ''What is it?''

''MR. COLTER?''

''Not now, Gem.''

''EMERGENCY ALERT AT SENIOR COLTER RESIDENCE.''

''Relay message,'' he snapped.

''Nick? It's your mother.'' Tension threaded her voice. ''There's been an accident in the lab. We need your help.''

''I'll be right there. Gem, monitor this link and contact

the police. I'll meet them outside my parents' house in ten minutes." He looked at Dani. "Will you still be here when I get back?"

"I don't know. I really don't know."

"For better or worse, they're my family. I have to go."

"I understand."

"This isn't over, Dani. If you're not here when I get back, I swear I'll track you down." And then he was gone.

Dani spent the next several hours trying to decide what course of action she should take. It bothered her horribly that Nick had lied, that he'd supported her financially for close to two years without telling her—and that he'd kept Peter's duplicity a secret. What chance did love have without honesty? The impulse to flee gripped her even more strongly than when Nick had first arrived on her doorstep. She felt a desperate urge to sort through what he'd told her. Most of all, she was driven to take control of her life.

She knew of only one place that could happen. She'd go to her parents and mull over her choices. They'd help her make sense of the situation, help her find a way through the tangle she'd made of her marriage.

She went to her bedroom and dressed. Then she dug a suitcase from beneath the jumble of boxes cluttering the bottom of her closet. She lugged it into Abbey's room and began throwing clothing into the cavernous depths.

"REQUEST INFORMATION," Gem interrupted.

Dani lifted her head from the drawer she was emptying. "What information?"

"CURRENT ACTIVITY NOT PART OF NORMAL ROUTINE. EXPLAIN ANOMALY."

"I'm packing."

"ONE MOMENT. ACCESSING." A minute later the computer came back on-line. "EXPLAIN REASON FOR PACKING."

"It's quite simple, Gem. Abbey and I are leaving."

"DESTINATION?"

Nosy computer. "Anywhere but here."

"TIME OF RETURN?"

"Never." She knelt on the floor and shoved a pile of diapers into the suitcase, muttering, "Process that, you deviating piece of mother board."

"ERROR NUMBER ZERO-ZERO-TWO."

"Wow. That must be one heck of an error to rate such a low number." Dani rocked on her heels. "What's an error number zero-zero-two?"

"EMERGENCY SITUATION IN PROGRESS."

She rose, planting her hands on her hips. "Now wait just one darn minute. What emergency is in progress?"

"DEVIATION REPORTED."

"I did not report a deviation, you mechanical hunk of junk. I'm leaving, not deviating!"

"ALL SYSTEMS RESPOND. FULL ALERT."

"Don't you dare call Nick! Are you listening to me?"

"COLTER OFF-LINE."

"Now, don't do anything stupid, Gem. This isn't the Toy Company, you know."

"PROCESSING. DEVIATION UNACCEPTABLE. FULL LOCK DOWN REQUIRED."

Panic stirred. "Stop it, Gem. There is no emergency in progress, and don't you *dare* lock anything down. Gem? Gem! Answer me, dammit! Abort lock down."

"REQUEST DENIED."

"I have level one security status. You can't deny my request."

"DEVIATION OVERRIDES LEVEL ONE SECURITY STATUS."

"Since when?"

"CORRECTION PROGRAMMED IN LAST TEN POINT FOUR SECONDS."

"Ten point—" Dani struggled to contain her fury. "You changed the rules ten point four seconds ago?"

"CURRENTLY, EIGHTEEN POINT TWO."

She ran to the door. Sure enough, it was locked. Next she tried to get out through the adjoining bathroom. The door leading to the hallway wouldn't budge, either. "You are one dead computer! Do you hear me, Gem?"

The only response was a halfhearted beep.

"Dani?" The house felt terminally empty, silent and depressing. Nick's back teeth clamped together. Hard. So, she'd left. He suspected she would. "Gem, status report."

"SECURITY ALERT," the computer whispered. "DEVIATION IN PROGRESS."

"Why the whisper mode, Gem?"

Silence met his question.

"Where's Dani?"

"MRS. COLTER WITH FEMALE OFFSPRING UNIT IN NURSERY."

She'd stayed? Relief hit like a body blow. He sprinted for Abigail's room, ramming into the door when the knob refused to yield to his touch. "What the hell?"

"Nick?"

"Why's the door locked, Dani?"

"Ask your damn computer!"

"Gem!"

"SECURITY ALERT. DEVIATION IN PROGRESS. FULL LOCK DOWN REQUIRED."

"*What?* Who ordered a full lock down?" Another

silence met his question. "Gem? Gem! Unlock the door."

"MRS. COLTER PACKING FOR UNKNOWN DESTINATION. RETURN DESIGNATION LISTED AS NEVER. THIS INFORMATION IS UNACCEPTABLE. FULL LOCK DOWN NECESSARY TO PREVENT OCCURRENCE CALLED LEAVING."

"Gem. You can't keep what you don't have. We can't force Dani to stay if she doesn't want to."

"LOCKED DOOR PREVENTS DEPARTURE."

He closed his eyes, leaning his forehead against the cool oak surface. "Unlock the door, Gem. Immediate compliance required."

Twenty full seconds passed before the lock was released. "COMPLIANCE GRANTED."

Dani opened the door. She held Abigail. Behind her he spotted a half-packed suitcase. "Hi, Nick."

"You're leaving." It wasn't a question.

"I'm trying."

"I didn't program her to prevent you."

"I know. She managed that one all on her own. I don't know how. But she did."

"She doesn't want you to leave." Taking a deep breath, he stepped into the room. He craved her, with every fiber of his being. He wanted to touch her, hold her, tie her up in so tight an embrace she'd never escape. But he couldn't. Dani had to make the decision to remain all by herself, without his pushing her into it. But words... He could use words, if nothing else. At least, he could try. "She's not the only one who wants you to stay. Don't do this, sweetheart. We can work through our problems if you'd stick it out and give our marriage half a chance."

"I can't," she whispered. "It's not that I'm not grateful. I am. I appreciate what you've tried to do. But I told you from the start that I can't survive another empty relationship. Not again. I need love, Nick. And I need someone who'll be honest. It won't work otherwise."

He searched desperately for leverage, seizing on the first thought that came to mind. "You promised a year. You promised to keep Abigail close by."

"I know. I won't go far." She hesitated, cocking her head. "Abigail. 'My father rejoices.' Did you know what that meant when you named her?"

Did she doubt it? Didn't she understand the significance? "I knew."

"Is that why you chose it?"

His hands collapsed into fists. "Do you have to ask?"

He caught the flash of anger in her night-black eyes, and it threw him. "I'd like you to tell me for once, instead of having to guess all the time." She paused. "But I suppose that's expecting too much. Would you carry my suitcase to the car?"

He ran a hand through his hair, swallowing his shout of refusal, forcing himself not to react, not to lose control. "Do I have any choice?"

"If you won't do it, I'll simply haul it down there myself."

He turned his thoughts inward, tapping into the source of his strength. It came more easily now, chilling his distress, blanketing his mind. "Don't bother. I'll take it."

Five minutes later they stood in front of the house. Nick loaded Abigail in her car seat while Dani tossed her keys from hand to hand. "I'll be at my parents' if you need to get in touch," she advised.

He straightened. It took every ounce of self-possession not to upend her across his shoulder and carry her back where she belonged. "Is there anything I can say to change your mind?"

She didn't answer immediately, but regarded him with steady dark eyes. At long last, she shook her head. "I guess not. The words don't seem to be in your vocabulary."

With that, Dani slid into the car. The engine roared to life and Nick turned. He refused to stand there like some poor lost soul and watch as his life drove away. He couldn't do it. Instead, he walked to the house.

He didn't look back.

Dani sat in the car and eyed Nick as he headed toward the front door. She released a pained sigh. Well, what did she expect? For him to suddenly admit to feelings he'd kept buried for thirty-five ice-cold years?

She thumped her fist against the steering wheel. Dammit! Why was the man so stubborn? Why couldn't he open his eyes and admit to loving his daughter? If he'd said even that much, she'd have relented. But if he couldn't admit to his feelings for one tiny baby, she didn't have a hope in hell of gaining that love for herself.

She threw the car into reverse, then hesitated. There was one question she'd like answered before she left. Earlier, she'd asked if he'd kept anything else from her. He'd said he had. She couldn't leave. Not yet. Not until she'd uncovered that one final secret. She shut off the engine and climbed from the car.

Nick walked into his office and stood in the middle of the room, not quite certain what to do next. It was an unpleasant experience. He'd never been at a loss before. There'd always been work. From the start, SSI had both captivated and driven him. But for some reason he'd lost that desire. It had vanished, along with Dani and Abigail.

He lowered his head, his muscles so taut they spasmed in protest. Why had Dani left? Didn't she realize how much a part of his life she and Abigail had become? Were the words that vital? Couldn't she sense what he'd been unable to say? Hear the words locked within him? Couldn't she see the yearning clawing for release?

He longed to walk into the nursery and find his daughter asleep in her crib. He longed to walk into the spare bedroom and find his wife arguing with Gem as she sorted through boxes. But most of all, he longed to walk into his own room and find Dani curled on top of their wedding sheets, her dark curls spilling across the ivory silk, her dusky eyes blinking at him with a seductive mixture of laughter and desire.

He heard a small sound behind him. A baby's whimper. He gritted his teeth, steeling himself for disappointment. Slowly, he turned. Dani stood there, holding Abigail. He opened his mouth to speak. To his shock, the words wouldn't come.

She didn't seem to notice. "I had to ask a question," she said in a rush. "Actually, I have two questions. I forgot to ask how your parents were doing. Are they okay?"

He nodded, finding his voice at last, although the words were low and rusty, rife with tension. "It was a false alarm. Dad spilled some chemicals and that caused the lab to automatically seal."

"I'm glad. Not about the chemical spill," she hastened to add. "Just that they're all right."

"I knew what you meant." He waited for her next question. When she hesitated, he prompted, "What else did you want to know?"

"Earlier, when I found out the truth about Peter, you mentioned there was something more you had to tell me. One final secret. I'd like to know what that is."

He steeled himself to answer, well aware that if he

hadn't lost her before, he would now. "You're not going to like it."

"I already suspected as much."

He didn't bother with tact but gave her the brutal, unvarnished truth. "I knew what Peter planned to do."

She stared at him in disbelief, the color seeping from her face. "You knew—"

"I knew, and I did absolutely nothing to stop him."

"Why?"

His mouth twisted. "Can't you guess?"

"You wanted full control of SSI?"

"Not even close."

"You wanted Peter out of your life?"

That struck him as funny, and he laughed, a harsh, grating sound that was short on humor and long on bitterness. "No, sweetheart. I wanted him out of yours."

He'd caught her by surprise. She gnawed at her lip, studying him with such a look of bewilderment that it tore at what passed for his heart. "I don't understand."

"Yes, you do. He was a rotten husband, Dani. He didn't love you. He didn't give you the care and attention you deserved. I wanted him to leave you. I made it easy for him."

"Why would you do that?"

He couldn't respond. Heaven help him, he wanted to. But he'd worked so hard, struggled for years to achieve control over his emotions. How could he explain feelings he'd spent five years denying, even to himself? The words didn't exist.

"Nick? Answer me. Why would you do that?"

He stared at her calmly. "You're right. I'm sorry. I had no business interfering."

She hesitated for a brief moment, and he knew she'd hoped for more. But his feelings remained locked away, buried far from reach. Finally, she inclined her head. "Thank you for being honest."

"You're leaving." *Say no! Tell me you'll stay!*

She nodded, and he caught the glint of tears. "Yes," she whispered. "I'm leaving."

"Because of a few words?" He took a step in her direction, then stopped. "Do you need to hear them that badly?"

"I'm afraid I do."

It was her turn to walk away. She pivoted and headed for the door. It slammed shut in her face, the lock snicking home.

"Dammit, Gem!" Nick roared in frustration. "Not again. Open the door!"

"NEGATIVE. UNAUTHORIZED DEPARTURE REFUSED."

"I'm authorizing her departure. Now unlock the door and let her go."

"UNABLE TO COMPLY."

"Why not?"

"MRS. COLTER WILL LEAVE."

The logic was indisputable, and his fury drained away. "Gem, you've been programmed to obey my orders. I'm ordering you to open the door."

"MRS. COLTER WILL LEAVE. WORDS ARE NECESSARY FOR MRS. COLTER AND FEMALE OFFSPRING UNIT TO STAY. GIVE REQUIRED WORDS."

He couldn't believe what he was hearing. "You want me to tell Dani I love her or you won't open the door?"

"ACCESSING. MRS. COLTER?"

Dani lifted her head, torn between laughter and tears. "Yes, Gem?"

"ARE WORDS 'I LOVE YOU' REQUIRED TO PREVENT DEPARTURE?"

The tears won, slipping down her cheeks. "Yes, Gem. They are. I need to know that he loves us. That he cares for us. That he'll never leave us."

"ACCESSING."

The bank of monitors behind Nick's desk sprang to life. Images filled the screen. Images of her with Abigail, images that spanned their two months of marriage. And then more images—images that spanned the five years of their partnership.

"What is this?" she asked, thoroughly confused.

The monitor went blank and then a single picture burst across the width of the screen. She recognized it as an incident that had taken place five years ago, not long after she'd gone to work at SSI. Peter had walked out of the room, leaving her alone with Nick. She'd been so intimidated by him, so awed by his intelligence and success, that she hadn't quite known what to do. In the video, Dani glanced at the notes she'd scribbled. She remembered focusing all her concentration on that silly pad because she'd been too nervous to speak. The camera switched to Nick.

He sat watching her. And the look on his face nearly destroyed her. It was filled with such hopeless longing that she began to weep.

"Delete image!" Nick bit the words out. "Now!"

"DELETING."

But in its place, another video clip appeared. Dear heavens. It was from the time she and Nick had been trapped in the closet while working together on the Kilburn contract. She was cradled in his arms, sound asleep. He held her, her head pillowed against his shoulder. And as she slept, he talked quietly, softly, a mere whisper of words. "I don't deserve you after some of the stunts I've pulled. But I swear on all I hold dear, I'll do whatever I can to protect you. I should let you go, let you get on with your life. But I can't. I need you, sweetheart. I always have and I guess I always will.''

Her knees buckled and Nick caught her, held her and Abigail tight within his arms. "Turn it off, Gem. Turn it off!''

"UNABLE TO COMPLY. WORDS NOT SPO-KEN.''

A final image blossomed to life. It must have been taped only moments before her return. Nick stood in the middle of his office, his head bowed, his hands locked into fists. On his face was a look of absolute agony.

Understanding struck with stunning force. "You can't say it, can you?" she whispered. "It isn't that you don't feel, you just can't express those feelings.''

"Dani, I—''

Prime the pump. She had to find a way to prime the pump.

Nick had told her how to do it. She remembered precisely what he'd said. To prime a pump you had to back feed water down the line to force out the air. Once the air bubble worked free, the water would start flowing. Which meant, if the words wouldn't come of their own volition, she'd need to start back feeding. She eased from his grasp and put Abbey on the couch, surrounding the baby with a bulwark of cushions. Then she returned to her husband and knelt at his side.

"Nick." She caught his face between her palms, forcing him to look at her.

"Please don't, Dani. No more.''

"Listen to me, my dearest husband. All these months, I've been waiting—waiting for you to say the words, for you to admit that you love me. And I suddenly realized, I've never said the words to you.'' Her hands slid through his blond-streaked hair, sinking into the crisp waves. "I love you. I love you with all my heart and soul. I have for a very long time."

The first crack appeared in his mask. His eyes blazed with fierce demand. "Don't leave, Dani. I'm not Peter. I swear I'm not."

"I know." She feathered her mouth across his, feeling his instant response. Hope soared. "I've been struggling to figure out why Peter left me destitute. He might have been a selfish man, but he wasn't cruel. I think... I think he did it because he suspected it would force your hand. You wouldn't have left me to struggle on my own. And Peter knew that."

Nick closed his eyes, the muscles in his face drawn taut. She could feel his heart pounding beneath her hands, feel as he gathered himself, like a runner faced with an impossible hurdle.

Finally he spoke. The words welled up, bursting through a lifetime of barriers. "I fell in love the first moment we met. It was wrong, and I knew it. But you were everything I ever dreamed a woman should be. I hated Peter for finding you before I had. And I hated how careless he was with your love." He opened his eyes. For the first time since she'd known him his gaze reflected peace, like a man who'd finally found salvation.

Her chin quivered. "Oh, Nick."

"You asked about Abigail's name. I owe you the truth about that." He cupped her face, his breath caressing her face, her lips, flooding her senses. "When I discovered you were pregnant, I couldn't believe it. I wanted a baby, a family. But I never expected to have one."

"Why?"

"Because..." He gathered her close, his mouth brushing hers as though he could gather strength from their kiss. "Because I never expected to marry."

"Why?" she asked again.

"Because the only woman I'd ever wanted was already taken." The words were so low, a mere whisper ripped from such a dark, secret place, she almost didn't hear. "Without you, marriage wasn't possible. Nor were children. When I found out you carried my baby, when you had my daughter..." He swallowed, shaking his head.

"You named her 'my father rejoices,'" Dani finished for him, tears spiking her lashes.

"I started celebrating the moment you opened the door and I saw your condition. Yeah, I rejoiced. You better believe I rejoiced. That baby offered me the chance for a birth, too. For a life I never dared dream was possible."

The tears slipped free. "Oh, Nick."

"Don't cry. Don't you get it? The two of you gave me a future. You gave me hope and love, something I'd never had before. Something I'd never expected to have." His gaze swept her face, offering an eternity of love and commitment. "I've waited so long for you. I've had so many empty yesterdays."

"Not anymore. We have today. And it's full. And we'll have tomorrow. And that will be even richer. I promise."

"I love you, sweetheart. I always have and I always will."

He claimed her with his mouth, claimed her as his mate, claimed her for all eternity. The shadows were gone from his heart and from his soul. He'd never again need to control his emotions, to hide behind cold, arctic barriers. Not any longer. He'd found salvation within the sweet embrace of his wife.

A satisfied beep echoed through the speakers.

"REQUESTED WORDS ACCESSED. FEMALE OFFSPRING UNIT NOT LEAVING. SECURITY ALERT CANCELED."

EPILOGUE

"IT'S A TRADITION, Gem. On the day of a person's birth everyone sings 'Happy Birthday.'"

"THIS IS THE BIRTH DAY OF MR. COLTER?"

Dani grinned as she lit the candles. "Affirmative."

"EXPLAIN SIGNIFICANCE OF CREATING FIRE HAZARD WITH BAKERY PRODUCT."

"It's a birthday cake and candles, Gem. Another tradition. I'm putting a candle on the cake for each of Nick's birthdays, plus one extra to grow on. Right now I'm lighting them. Next we'll sing, then Nick will make a wish and blow out the candles. That's how it's done."

"WISH IS NECESSARY TO SUCCESSFULLY EXTINGUISH FLAMES?"

"Absolutely. The order is crucial."

"ONE-YEAR ANNIVERSARY FOR BIRTH OF FEMALE OFFSPRING UNIT WILL OCCUR IN THIRTY-TWO-POINT-FOUR DAYS. WILL BIRTHDAY TRADITION BE OBSERVED AGAIN?"

"Sure will. Of course, Abbey will need help blowing out her candles. She's still a little too young to do it by herself. But she'll learn."

After lighting the final candle, Dani whisked the cake off the counter and carried it into the dining room. Instantly, her relatives burst into song. She watched a slow grin appear on Nick's face and realized with a pang how much he'd come to appreciate the endless bounty of her family's affections. It still hurt to think about the dearth of love and attention he'd suffered during his childhood. And though he'd come to terms with his parents' inability to provide for his needs, she knew how he longed to experience the sort of unconditional affection she'd enjoyed. Fortunately, her relatives were all too happy to step into the breach and embrace a new family member.

A stack of presents filled the table in front of him, but she knew what meant the most was that his in-laws had taken the time and trouble to choose something specially for him.

Nick caught her by the waist and tipped her into his lap. Ignoring the laughter and catcalls, Dani wrapped her arms around his neck. "Happy birthday," she murmured, giving him a lingering kiss.

Determined not to miss out, Abbey climbed aboard with a loud, "Up!" and gave her parents enthusiastic chocolate kisses from a frosting-coated mouth. To Dani's delight, Nick didn't pull back or attempt to avoid his daughter's embrace. Instead, he gave her a loving hug and tucked her close.

"Thank you for arranging all this, by the way," he said in an undertone.

"I'd have been in serious trouble with Ruth if I hadn't."

"Why?"

She offered a gentle smile. "You're family now. If I hadn't included them tonight, I'd have been stealing a memory."

He didn't reply for a moment, and she suspected he still had trouble coming to terms with his importance in the family structure. But he was learning. Slowly but surely, he'd opened up, rarely retreating into ice mode. She sensed the need in him far outweighed the wariness—the fear that this would all end tomorrow.

"They didn't have to bring gifts," he said gruffly.

"Sure they did. It's tradition." She dropped her head

to his shoulder and ruffled Abbey's auburn curls. "Tell me what you wished for."

"Isn't it supposed to be a secret?"

"Not from your wife. Now, what was it?"

"I wished...." He leaned closer, his mouth touching the curve of her ear and stirring the fine hair at her temple. "I wished for another picture for your grandmother's locket."

It only took a moment for comprehension to set in. "A brother or sister for Abbey?"

"Is it too soon? Our work load has eased off. Thanks to Raven Sierra, our domestic sales are through the ceiling."

"We can move those decimal points over?" she teased, recalling Hugh's comment at dinner that long-ago night. "You're not just a measly old millionaire anymore?"

"Not for much longer."

"I'll tell you what. Why don't we discuss this further after the party?"

Nick's eyes darkened to indigo. "Promise?"

"Absolutely. After all, it's a birthday wish. And in case you didn't know, those always come true."

"WISH IS NECESSARY TO SUCCESSFULLY EXTINGUISH FLAMES," Gem announced.

River Sierra nodded solemnly, studying the birthday cake her housekeeper had placed on the table. "That's what I thought. It won't work if I don't wish first. Right?"

"AFFIRMATIVE."

She eyed her father's present—another Jack Rabbitt storybook filled with the most beautiful pictures she'd ever seen. He'd even bought one of the paintings from the book and hung it on her bedroom wall. River loved the painting, loved it with all the passion her five-year-old body could summon. It was of a fairy riding a butterfly, a fairy with long black hair, just like hers. In the book, the fairy could grant wishes, and River had a very special wish.

"HAS WISH BEEN MADE?" Gem inquired.

"Not yet."

"DANGER OF FIRE HAZARD IMMINENT."

"What?"

"HURRY."

"Oh. Okay. I'm hurrying." River squeezed her eyes shut and then whispered, "I want a mommy for my very own. And I want her to be just like the fairy in my painting." With that, she opened her eyes and blew out the candles.

It was done. She'd made her wish. Now she just had to wait for it to come true. Because Gem had told her...

Birthday wishes always came true.

* * * * *

*Find out what happens to Raven, River and Gem
in* The Miracle Wife, *coming in the fall!*

But, first in June...Look for Day Leclaire's
The Boss, the Baby and the Bride,
*part of Harlequin Romance's Guardian Angel
promotion.*

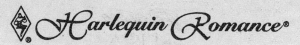

Harlequin Romance®

Invites You to A Wedding!

Whirlwind Weddings
Combines the heady romance of a whirlwind courtship with the excitement of a wedding— strong heroes, feisty heroines and marriages made not so much in heaven as in a hurry!

What's the catch? All our heroes and heroines meet and marry within a week! Mission impossible? Well, a lot can happen in seven days....

January 1998—#3487 MARRY IN HASTE
by Heather Allison

February 1998—#3491 DASH TO THE ALTAR
by Ruth Jean Dale

March 1998—#3495 THE TWENTY-FOUR-HOUR BRIDE
by Day Leclaire

April 1998—#3499 MARRIED IN A MOMENT
by Jessica Steele

Who says you can't hurry love?

Available wherever Harlequin books are sold.

Look for these titles—
available at your favorite retail outlet!

January 1998
Renegade Son by Lisa Jackson
Danielle Summers had problems: a rebellious child
and unscrupulous enemies. In addition, her Montana
ranch was slowly being sabotaged. And then there was
Chase McEnroe—who admired her land and desired her
body. But Danielle feared he would invade more than just
her property—he'd trespass on her heart.

February 1998
The Heart's Yearning by Ginna Gray
Fourteen years ago Laura gave her baby up for adoption,
and not one day had passed that she didn't think about
him and agonize over her choice—so she finally followed
her heart to Texas to see her child. But the plan to watch
her son from afar doesn't quite happen that way, once the
boy's sexy—*single*—father takes a decided interest in *her*.

March 1998
First Things Last by Dixie Browning
One look into Chandler Harrington's dark eyes and
Belinda Massey could refuse the Virginia millionaire nothing.
So how could the no-nonsense nanny believe the rumors that
he had kidnapped his nephew—an adorable, healthy little boy
who crawled as easily into her heart as he did into her lap?

BORN IN THE USA: Love, marriage—
and the pursuit of family!

Look us up on-line at: http://www.romance.net

BUSA4

Don't miss these Harlequin favorites by some of our top-selling authors!

HT#25733	THE GETAWAY BRIDE by Gina Wilkins	$3.50 U.S. ☐ $3.99 CAN. ☐	
HP#11849	A KISS TO REMEMBER by Miranda Lee	$3.50 U.S. ☐ $3.99 CAN. ☐	
HR#03431	BRINGING UP BABIES by Emma Goldrick	$3.25 U.S. ☐ $3.75 CAN. ☐	
HS#70723	SIDE EFFECTS by Bobby Hutchinson	$3.99 U.S. ☐ $4.50 CAN. ☐	
HI#22377	CISCO'S WOMAN by Aimée Thurlo	$3.75 U.S. ☐ $4.25 CAN. ☐	
HAR#16666	ELISE & THE HOTSHOT LAWYER by Emily Dalton	$3.75 U.S. ☐ $4.25 CAN. ☐	
HH#28949	RAVEN'S VOW by Gayle Wilson	$4.99 U.S. ☐ $5.99 CAN. ☐	

(limited quantities available on certain titles)

AMOUNT	$ _____
POSTAGE & HANDLING	$ _____
($1.00 for one book, 50¢ for each additional)	
APPLICABLE TAXES*	$ _____
TOTAL PAYABLE	$ _____

(check or money order—please do not send cash)

To order, complete this form and send it, along with a check or money order for the total above, payable to Harlequin Books, to: **In the U.S.:** 3010 Walden Avenue, P.O. Box 9047, Buffalo, NY 14269-9047; **In Canada:** P.O. Box 613, Fort Erie, Ontario, L2A 5X3.

Name: _____

Address: _____ City: _____

State/Prov.: _____ Zip/Postal Code: _____

Account Number (if applicable): _____

*New York residents remit applicable sales taxes.
Canadian residents remit applicable GST and provincial taxes.

Look us up on-line at: http://www.romance.net

075-CSAS

HBLJM98